A Horse Called Holiday

Frances Wilbur

AN
APPLE
PAPERBACK

SCHOLASTIC INC.
New York Toronto London Auckland Sydney

TO MARGUERITE CREAMER PEARSON,
our beloved Aunt Margo,
who kept telling me this was a good story

No part of this publication may be reproduced in whole or in part, or stored in a retrieval system, or transmitted in any form or by any means, electronic, mechanical, photocopying, recording, or otherwise, without written permission of the publisher. For information regarding permission, write to Scholastic Inc., 730 Broadway, New York, NY 10003.

ISBN 0-590-44548-0

12 11 10 9 8 7 6 5 4 3   3 4 5 6 7/9

Printed in the U.S.A.   28

First Scholastic printing, December 1992

Contents

1. Middie, the Caboose   1
2. A Horse for Halsey's Grandson   10
3. Blue Paint   18
4. At the Dinner Table   23
5. Janet   29
6. Happy Holiday   36
7. A Big Mistake   45
8. The Discovery   53
9. From Despair to Delight   64
10. Not Holiday. No.   71
11. Val Verde, Here I Come   78
12. The Awful Birthday Party   84
13. Horse Show Rules   91
14. Val Verde After All   97
15. Tyler, Mike, and Susie   104
16. Junior Jumpers   110
17. Over the Fence and Out   118
18. The Ditch Jump   127
19. A Stomachache   134
20. Holiday Attacks   139
21. Decisions, Decisions   145

22. Highgate Hills Farm 155
23. Middie Calls a Bluff 161
24. The Right Choice 167
25. Derry Gets Even 175
26. The Long Night 183
27. The Fox Hunt 193

1.
Middie, the Caboose

The voice on the loudspeaker carried clearly over the brightly painted red, white, and blue jumps in the ring, over the crowded grandstands, over the parking lots with their rows and rows of cars.

Sunlight gleamed softly on the velvet hunt caps and polished boots of the young riders in the arena as they sat on their braided horses, motionless, waiting, expectant.

"The winner of the Idlewood Junior Jumping Championship is" — in the pause that followed, even the horses seemed to be listening — "Meredith Scott, on Bugle Boy."

Middie's heart bounced back into place and started beating again. At the roar of applause she smiled and picked up Bugle Boy's reins. She tried to look nonchalant as she rode toward the group of officials.

How much she had wanted this! How proud her family would be! Proud of *me*, Middie Scott, she

1

told herself. Winner of the Idlewood Junior Jumping Championship!

She glanced at the faces of the Riding Club kids down the line. She saw envy and disappointment, and a few showed admiration. She had beaten them all, even Tyler Benning! Tyler tossed her head and looked away as Middie rode past.

In the center a man held a streamer of multicolored ribbons and an enormous silver bowl, ornately engraved. It glittered in the sun.

Far away in the parking lot someone was honking a horn.

That bowl is huge! thought Middie. Bigger than all of Laurie's tennis trophies put together. I wonder what Mom and Dad will say.

"Congratulations, Meredith," said the man holding the silver bowl. He was bald with a fringe of white hair circling his pink dome. Middie knew he was the president of the Idlewood Club.

Middie halted her big bay horse, and the president looked up at her. "You must be the youngest rider ever to win the Junior Championship!" he exclaimed.

"I'm twelve," Middie said. "I'm in seventh grade."

The president smiled broadly. "May I call you Middie?" he asked. "I've heard that's your nickname." He held up the bowl with two hands so Middie could put one hand on it and pose. The honking horn grew more insistent. "Smile," said the president. The photographer aimed his camera, and another man waved a crumply sheet of white paper to make Bugle Boy prick his ears. Middie smiled.

"Meredith Scott, what in the *world* are you *DOING*?" shouted her sister's voice.

Middie blinked. She wasn't at the Idlewood Horse Show. She was sitting on Mrs. Jamison's palomino mare, Peaches, in Mrs. Jamison's back-yard, wearing blue jeans and a white T-shirt that read, "Lord give me patience. Right now." Some post-and-rail jumps needing paint were lined up near the fence.

Middie looked around. Her sister Laurie had parked behind the barn and was leaning out of the car window.

"You're sitting there like you're having your picture taken, and you're smiling, just SMIL-ING," said Laurie, "while I was honking and yell-ing my head off."

"Oh," said Middie. "I was thinking of some-thing."

"Well, I guess!" Laurie made a face. "You were supposed to clean the patio this morning, remem-ber? You rushed off without thinking, as usual."

"Oh," said Middie again. "I'm sorry." It seemed to her she spent most of her life saying she was sorry.

Laurie sighed. "Well, go on home and clean it up before you do anything else. Before I pick Mom up from work. She was really mad this morning."

"Okay. I'm almost through." Middie shifted the

reins, and the horse pricked her ears. "Do you want to watch me?"

"No, I've got . . . oh, well, I guess so."

Middie trotted the palomino around the big yard, turned, and cantered toward the line of fences. The mare jumped smoothly over the first three, picked up speed, flew over the fourth fence, and bolted.

"She's getting better," yelled Middie, hauling on the reins. "She used to bolt after the first fence."

"I remember." Laurie watched in silence until Middie circled the horse. "I don't know why you keep riding her."

"I get paid," said Middie. "I'm going to buy my own horse. Besides, I want to enter Peaches in the Idlewood show, and I'm going to win, too." Middie trotted up to the fence in time to hear Laurie mutter, "Oh, geez. Miss Show-off again."

Middie frowned. "I *will* win. If I can't win this year, I'll win next year."

Laurie rolled her eyes. "Okay, Caboose. Just don't forget the patio." The car backed down the drive.

Caboose. That did it. Middie groaned and began to trot the horse briskly around the yard.

She hated being called Caboose. She hated being reminded that she was born nearly six years after the others. There were Keith and Karen and Laurie, close together, and then, six years later, Middie. "The little surprise," her mother always said, smiling, but Middie noticed nobody else smiled. Laurie called her the Caboose — the end of the train after all the important cars.

"The tail end of the family," she muttered. "I'm not the little surprise; I'm the big mistake. It's not *my* fault I came along when I did." The horse trotted faster.

"And everybody thinks Laurie's so great because she wins trophies in her dumb old tennis tournaments. Well, someday I'll win more trophies in jumping classes than Laurie has ever won." Middie's voice trembled. "Then they'll be glad I'm in the family."

The horse tossed her head and broke into a canter. "And Mom will say, 'Why, Middie, we didn't know you could ride like that. We're awfully proud of you.' " Peaches suddenly jerked the reins and tried to bolt.

Middie sank into the saddle and concentrated on the horse. They slowed to a trot. "I'm sorry," Middie said, stroking the mare's neck gently. "They'll see," she told Peaches. "Mom keeps telling me I don't have to win anything, but how else can I make them proud of me like they are of Laurie?" The arena blurred. "I'll show them. I *will* do something special."

The most special thing she knew was the Idlewood Junior Jumping Championship, but how could she enter when she didn't even have a horse? She just hoped Peaches would be good enough by then. Middie sighed deeply and draped herself over Peaches, one arm dangling on either side of the horse's neck.

The mare's coat was golden, like sliced peaches, her mane and tail the color of cream poured over them. Middie buried her face in the flaxen mane and took a deep breath. The mane smelled faintly of shampoo and clean horse, and Middie was partly comforted.

The sound of a car on the driveway made her sit up. It was Laurie again. She put her head out the window. "I almost forgot. Mrs. Bailey called. She wants you to come over early. She has something to show you."

Middie wiped her face quickly on one arm and galloped up to the fence. "What does she want to show me? Why didn't you tell me?"

"I don't know what it is and I *am* telling you." Laurie sighed. "But you've got to clean the patio before you go there. For once, don't be a pain." She drove away again.

Middie stared after the car. "You're not my mother," she said loudly. "I'll go to Mrs. Bailey's first if I want to." She began walking the horse slowly around the arena to cool her off.

Mrs. Bailey was the only grown-up Middie knew who understood Middie's love of horses. Mrs. Bailey was very old and hadn't ridden for years, but at her home she still kept her favorite horse. He was an ancient gray hunter named Londonderry Aire. Middie took care of Derry, fed him twice a day, and mucked out his stall. She would have done it for nothing because she wanted to be with horses, but Mrs. Bailey said no, Middie ought to be paid, and she paid Middie well.

"You want a horse?" Mrs. Bailey had said in a brisk voice. "Well, don't just ask for one. Open a savings account and save up for it."

Middie did, thinking that it would take forever, but it was her only hope. Three years ago, when Middie first announced at home that she wanted a horse, her father had burst out laughing. He said, "You can't even take care of your room; how could you take care of a horse?"

Her mother didn't think it was funny. "Please be *reasonable*, Middie," she said, little worry lines between her eyebrows. "Horses are terribly expensive. With your brother still in college, and Laurie starting soon, a horse is impossible. That's one expense we can't have."

But when Mrs. Bailey had found several other stable jobs for her, Middie was surprised at how fast her savings account grew. Middie was going to keep her horse at Mrs. Bailey's when she finally got one.

"Peaches, what do you suppose she wants to show me?" she asked the mare as they stopped by the barn. "I'll bet it's a horse, but whose?"

Middie swung to the ground and unhooked her helmet. She pulled it off, shaking her head. The helmet was hot and sweaty, and the wind felt good in her short brown hair. Middie knew she looked better with long hair because she was tall and thin, but long hair was a lot of trouble.

Her hair had been long until last month. She had cut it herself the day she was jumping Peaches and her hair fell down from her helmet, into her eyes. She couldn't see where she was going, and almost crashed into a fence. As soon as she had put the horse away, she got out the horse clippers and cut her hair.

Back home, her mother had walked in the kitchen door, gasped, and collapsed onto the nearest chair.

"Oh, Middie, how could you! Your lovely brown hair!" She rubbed her forehead. "Why do you always have to rush off and do something right away without thinking? If you'd only waited, I could have made an appointment for you."

Middie shrugged. "My hair got in my eyes."

Her mother groaned and went to the telephone. The next day, Middie had to go to the hair salon to have her hair evened up. It wasn't the world's greatest haircut, but it was a lot better for riding.

Middie arranged the bridle on its hook and slid the saddle onto the rack. "Maybe it's a horse that somebody can't ride. When he sees how well I ride him, he'll give the horse to me." This was Middie's second favorite daydream, after the one of winning at Idlewood.

She quickly threw some hay into the manger, turned the mare loose, and gave her a piece of carrot from her jeans pocket. "Peaches, I've GOT to find out what Mrs. Bailey wants to show me."

She ran to the bicycle parked under the big eucalyptus tree, hopped on, and scooted down the driveway.

2.
A Horse for Halsey's Grandson

Middie always had to pump hard to get up the hill to Mrs. Bailey's house. She usually arrived in a state of near-exhaustion, but today the hills didn't seem so steep, nor the distance so long. She got off and pushed the bike up the winding driveway and leaned it against the fence.

Mrs. Bailey lived at the edge of town in an enormous house of weathered gray clapboard on top of the highest hill. With its gray shingled roof, elaborate carved eaves, and three round turrets, it looked to Middie like a storybook castle. At the foot of the hill leaned an old gray barn, surrounded on three sides by a row of fenced paddocks, a field obviously used as a riding ring, and a large pasture.

"I knew you'd be early," said Mrs. Bailey, climbing carefully down the steps from the front porch. One hand held on to the railing, the other on to a cane. The old lady looked frail enough to be blown away by a brisk wind, but one thin hand grasped the cane firmly. Her snow-white hair was gathered into a big bun at the back of her head. Her eyes were gray and lively in a face as weathered as her house.

Middie exclaimed, "Mrs. Bailey, you're not supposed to go down those steps alone! Why didn't you wait for me, or else go around the back way?"

"Balderdash," said Mrs. Bailey. "Do you remember Halsey, the old horse trader who comes around now and then?"

"You mean the old guy who remembers every horse he ever met, and can't remember where he parked his truck?" Middie rolled her eyes. "Who could forget him!"

"He bought a horse at the Pomona auction for his grandson. He's keeping the horse here until the boy's birthday in a couple of months. You can ride the horse as much as you want in exchange for taking care of him."

Middie whooped. "That's like having my own horse!"

Mrs. Bailey nodded.

"Oh, wow!" shouted Middie. "What's he like?"

"He's an older horse, but he's pretty lively. I hope Halsey's grandson is a good rider."

"Let's go look!" Middie tucked Mrs. Bailey's thin arm in hers. She wanted to run, but she made herself walk slowly along the path to the barn.

"What kind of a horse is he?" Middie asked. "What's his name?"

"He's a thoroughbred." The old lady shook her head. "I forgot to ask his name."

As they came down the path, a big gray horse poked his head out of the barn. That was Derry. Half a minute later, a second head appeared from the other stall.

Middie drew in her breath.

He was a brilliant chestnut — the color of burnished copper. His eyes, set in a broad forehead, were bold and dark and shining. His head was straight and slender, with nostrils like sculptured crescents. In the center of his forehead was a white star, diamond-shaped with a curlicue at the lower corner. He stood motionless and silent while his dark eyes followed her.

Middie walked slowly toward the horse and stopped in front of his stall. His nostrils flared without a sound; there was no other movement. Middie felt a little shiver run up her spine.

"Oh, Mrs. Bailey," whispered Middie. "*Look* at him!"

"Well, he's quite a horse. Be careful when you bring him out. Let's see what you think."

Without warning, the thoroughbred stiffened, flattened his ears, and blew loudly through his nostrils.

Middie jumped but stayed. She felt in her pocket and cautiously held out a piece of carrot on the palm of her hand. "You sure are handsome," she said quietly. "We're going to be friends, you and me." She stood very still, palm outstretched, talking softly. The horse didn't move.

Middie reached out with her other hand and touched his shoulder with her fingertips. Slowly she ran her hand up his neck, rubbing in little circles with her fingers.

The horse looked at her warily. Middie could tell from his breathing and stiffness that he was frightened. She could even feel his heart thumping hard against his ribs.

"He's scared to death!" Middie exclaimed.

"Yes, I know." Mrs. Bailey frowned. "Last night I heard some noise in the stables. I went to see what was going on, and he was stomping and drenched in sweat — almost as if he were having a bad dream."

Middie turned once again to the horse. "Don't be frightened," she said in a low, calm voice. "Nothing bad will happen to you now you're here." But he didn't respond except to strain his head forward as if trying to hear her.

She kept stroking him gently, and suddenly the horse let out the breath he had been holding in a long drawn-out sigh. He flicked his ears forward and carefully picked up the carrot. Middie could hear him crunch it in his back teeth.

"Whew!" said Middie. She scratched along the crest of his neck toward his ears. The horse took another deep breath and lowered his head.

Middie smiled. "How come you're so suspicious?" she asked. She held out another carrot. "Has somebody been mean to you?"

The horse picked up the carrot and munched it, studying the girl. Then he put his head against her shoulder and began to rub it up and down. Middie laughed.

"I guess he's going to like me," she said, "but he wasn't sure at first."

Mrs. Bailey nodded. "His halter is on the peg beside Derry's. Why don't you turn him out in the field? It will be good for him, and we can see what he's like."

He held his head down for the halter, and Middie led him past Derry's paddock and into the field. Derry followed on his side of the fence, glaring across at the new horse and challenging him to battle. In the field, Middie unsnapped the horse's lead rope and stepped back.

The chestnut horse chose to ignore the gray hunter. He blew fiercely again, then trotted with floating steps alongside the high wooden fence, his neck arched, his nostrils wide, and his tail like a flag in a high wind. He suddenly trumpeted and began rearing and leaping and bucking. He bucked three times in a row and then reared straight up, striking at an imaginary enemy. Down to earth he came, bucked once more, and went into a wild gallop around the entire field. His body seemed to lengthen, and his powerful legs took enormous strides.

"He looks like a racehorse!" exclaimed Middie.

"He probably was. A horse who's been on the track never forgets how to run." They watched in silence for a minute.

The open field stretched before the horse like the racetracks he had known. On the track he had been called Magic, although his registered name was Mostly Magic. As his pounding hooves cut into the hard ground, his body throbbed with familiar excitement.

Middie said, "It's almost as if the earth itself is telling him to run. Isn't he great?"

Mrs. Bailey nodded. "He reminds me of Derry, long before he rolled down the mountainside with me."

"Derry was like *that*?" She couldn't imagine the easygoing gray hunter with the permanent limp racing around the field like the chestnut horse. She glanced quickly at Derry, snorting in his paddock. She wondered how he must feel to see another horse galloping as he used to.

Mrs. Bailey frowned. "It's a good thing that fence is five feet high. We built it so Derry wouldn't go over the top of it. I hope it will keep this horse in."

Middie turned quickly. "You mean this horse can jump?"

"Didn't I tell you? Must have slipped my mind."

"Mrs. Bailey, that's what I love most of all!"

"It is?" The corners of her mouth twitched. "Well, yes. Halsey said he was a jumper."

"A jumper! Wow!" Middie felt as though she were in one of her daydreams. "When can I start riding him?"

"Why not tomorrow? You'll probably want to work him on a lunge line first."

"Sure thing!" exclaimed Middie. "I'll do my other stables first so I can stay here."

"Well, better cool him out now and put him away, or you'll be late for dinner."

"Dinner!" Middle clapped one hand to her forehead. "Oh, no! I forgot I have to clean the patio before Mom gets home!"

The horse ignored her whistles and calls until he turned and caught sight of her. He stopped, then trotted slowly toward her. He wasn't hard to catch, but he was too excited to be led at a walk. Middie braced herself against him to keep him from jigging sideways. At last she cooled him enough to put him away.

She pedaled home furiously, hoping her mother and Laurie hadn't gotten there yet.

They lived in an older section of town in a Spanish bungalow of tan stucco with a red tiled roof and a picturesque courtyard in front, enclosed by a low wall and an archway. A long time ago, the only houses on the block were Spanish bungalows like theirs, surrounded by big lawns. Then some developers had built modern frame houses in between the Spanish stuccos. Instead of lawns, the houses were now separated by thin strips of cement driveways.

Middie liked their old Spanish house much better than any of the new houses, but her mother said she would gladly trade the romantic courtyard for a modern kitchen any day.

Middie was pedaling up the driveway when she heard the telephone ring.

3.
Blue Paint

The telephone kept on ringing. Middie dropped her bike and ran inside to answer it.

"I'm glad you're home," said her mother's voice. "I just wanted to let you know I'm running late."

"That's okay."

"Have you finished the patio?"

"I, ah, I'm working on it," said Middie.

"Thank goodness. See you in a little while."

How lucky could she get! She hung up and glanced into the mirror above the telephone table. Her face was covered with dirt except for one clean streak where she had wiped it on her T-shirt. She went in to the bathroom and turned on the faucets.

Middie wished her face wasn't so thin, or else her mouth wasn't so wide. They didn't quite go together, but her nose was okay. Her father kept saying she would have to be careful with those deep blue eyes when she got older. If that meant she might have to wear glasses, it would be murder for riding. She sighed, finished washing up, and went through the hallway to the patio.

It wasn't really a patio anymore. It was enclosed like a regular room with big windows, hardwood floors, and a slanting ceiling, more like a glassed-in porch. It was Middie's favorite room.

At the door to the patio she winced.

It was worse than she remembered. Paint-splashed newspapers covered the floor, and everywhere were scattered pencils, brushes, sketch pads, and paints of every color, in tubes and jars and boxes. In the center of the room rose a large easel with a half-finished painting of galloping horses, heads high and manes and tails flying as they raced through tall green grass.

Middie tilted her head slightly at the picture and squinted her eyes to blot out the unfinished background. "Not bad," she muttered. She unsquinted, sighed deeply, and began gathering the paints and papers.

Her family wasn't very enthusiastic about her painting.

"You don't take time to paint things as well as you could," her mother told her.

And Laurie complained, "All you ever draw is horses."

It wasn't true. In her room, Middie was secretly working on a painting that didn't have a single horse in it. Middie knew it was one of the best things she'd done — a landscape of the tree-lined canyon leading to the mountains in back of Mrs. Bailey's house. When Middie looked at it, it made her want to hike up the trail and see what was around the bend. Middie was going to give it to Laurie for her eighteenth birthday next month.

She wanted Laurie to like it a lot. Laurie had never come right out and blamed Middie for not having a room of her own all those years, but Middie was sure that's how Laurie felt. It wasn't until Karen went away to college that Laurie got her own room again. Middie imagined how good the picture would look over Laurie's desk.

Sometimes Middie thought her mother really admired her painting, but it seemed as if anything that started out as a compliment ended up as a criticism. Like saying her horses were good, but she always put them in tall grass so she wouldn't have to draw their hooves right. Middie fixed her eyes on the galloping horses on the painting on the easel. She hated drawing hooves. She muttered, "Everybody knows horses like to run in tall grass."

She sorted tubes and brushes while her mind explored the possibilities of the new horse. She wondered how difficult he would be to ride. What a beauty he was! Maybe she could enter him in a horse show before Halsey took him away. If only she could have a horse like that for her very own.

She imagined herself riding out of the ring with blue ribbons in her hand, giving them to her mother at the gate. Laurie's face would be one big "oh" of surprise. Her mother would look astonished and proud. Her father would look happy and say . . .

With a start, she looked at the room. She knew just what her mother would say if she found it like this. Middie jammed the discarded papers into a cardboard box and carried it out to the garage. On her way back she glanced at the kitchen clock. Where had the time gone? Thank heavens her mother and Laurie were late. She hastily began throwing the things she wanted to save into another box.

She heard a thump and a splash. Bright blue tempera paint poured out onto the shining hardwood floor in a widening pool.

"I was sure I put that lid on tight!" moaned Middie. "My brand-new blue, a whole jar!" She grabbed some rags and began mopping, but that only made it worse.

A horn went *beep beep beep* loudly just outside the house.

That sounds like our car, thought Middie. Oh, good grief, I bet I left my bike in the driveway! She threw the dripping rags into the trash box and looked frantically around the room. If her mother saw this, Middie wouldn't get to ride for a month!

Newspapers! They would have to do. She grabbed several sections, opened them up, and spread them out flat over the spilled paint. On inspiration she pulled the braided rugs over the newspapers. She could clean it up later, and no one would ever know.

"I'm coming!" she yelled, and raced outside to where she had left the bicycle. She could hardly wait to tell her family about her new horse.

4.
At the Dinner Table

Sure enough, there was the car, with Laurie behind the wheel and her mother beside her, and there was the bike, in the middle of the driveway. Middie dragged it off into the grass. "Well, it was almost off the drive," she said, bracing herself for the lecture. This definitely was not the time to mention the new horse.

Laurie smiled. "That's okay, Middie. I guess today is a rush day for everybody."

Middie stared after her as the car pulled into the garage. Maybe she's not feeling well, thought Middie. She leaned the bike up against the house. "Hi, Mom," she said. "Did you have a good day?"

Her mother kissed her cheek lightly. "Pretty good. How was yours?"

"Fine. I . . ."

Laurie said mildly, "Why don't you put your bike in the garage?" She lifted a sack of groceries out of the car and started toward the house. She had been playing tennis, and her short white skirt swung in rhythm with her slender brown legs.

Laurie was seventeen, almost eighteen, and seemed very grown-up to Middie, most of the time. She had blonde hair that reached below her shoulders, and she was small and curved and neat. Middie was thin as a rail, already three inches taller than Laurie, and she felt herself growing taller every day, like Alice in Wonderland after swallowing the pill that said, "Eat me."

Middie sighed. "Okay." She pushed the bike into the garage and followed them into the house.

"Did you get the patio clean?" asked her mother. She was putting away the groceries.

"I'm practically through."

"I'll help you finish," said Laurie.

"That's okay," Middie said hastily. She hurried to the patio.

Laurie came after her and paused in the doorway. "Well, it looks fine to me. What more do you have to do?"

Middie cleared her throat. "Nothing, I guess, except take those boxes to my room." She picked up a box and looked at her sister. "Did you and David have a fight or something?"

Laurie shook her head. "No. We were playing tennis. Why?"

"I dunno," said Middie. Whenever Laurie was very nice to Middie, she'd either had a fight with her boyfriend, or else she wanted something. The rest of the time Laurie just put up with her.

Middie couldn't really blame her. Middie figured

out that everything in the family changed when Middie was born.

Middie carried the boxes to her room and put them down on the floor near a pile of jeans, T-shirts, and underpants. Plastic models of horses covered the top of her dresser. On the wall hung various horse posters, and one of the Statue of Liberty pointing a finger, saying, "Keep America beautiful. Pick up your clothes."

Middie thought a moment. Maybe right after dinner, when everybody was relaxed and happy, would be the best time to tell about her horse. Her mom and dad liked to have a second cup of coffee and sit and talk.

After they sat down at the table, Laurie turned to Middie. "Will you be ready to go by eight-thirty?"

Middie looked blank.

"To the beach tomorrow," said Laurie patiently. "You and Janet are going with us, remember?"

Middie groaned. David's cousin, Janet, was spending the summer with his family while her parents were on a business trip. Middie had completely forgotten she had promised to go to the beach with them. "I can't go to the beach. I'm going to Mrs. Bailey's. It wasn't *my* idea to invite David's cousin to spend the summer here."

Laurie's voice rose. "You promised. Janet is counting on it. She hasn't been to the beach yet."

Middie shook her head vigorously. "But that was before I got the new horse."

"What new horse?" thundered her father.

"He's not really mine," said Middie hastily. "He belongs to Halsey, but he's at Mrs. Bailey's for a couple of months. While he's there, I get to ride him like he's my own. Janet can go to the beach without me."

"There you go again," said Laurie, "messing up everybody's plans at the last minute. Janet needs somebody her own age to hang out with, and you said you'd go."

Middie said, "You don't care about Janet; you just don't want her hanging around you and David."

"What's wrong with that?" asked Laurie. "When you're grown-up, you'll feel the same way." Middie heard her mutter under her breath, "If you ever do grow up."

"Wait a minute," said Middie, brightening. "Janet likes horses. She's got one of her own. I can ask her if she'd rather go to Mrs. Bailey's with me. She'd probably be glad to see the new horse."

Her mother looked at Middie. "If you promised to go to the beach, you ought to stick to it. Besides, it would be good for you to have a change from riding. I'm sure Janet is looking forward to seeing the Pacific Ocean."

"I didn't really promise; I just said I'd go. And she *lives* on the beach in Connecticut with the ocean right in front. Big deal. What's the difference between oceans?"

"The whole United States," said her father. He smiled.

"Ha!" said Middie. Then, "I'll talk to Janet. She's only been here a week. She's got the rest of the summer to see the ocean."

"Well, David and I are definitely going. I have to get rid of my tennis tan lines."

"Why don't you wear your bikini to play tennis in?" asked Middie. "Then you wouldn't have to go to the beach at all."

Her father smiled. "Now there's a good suggestion."

Laurie rolled her eyes. "But if Janet wants to go to the beach, you've got to come along."

"She won't." Middie put her chin up. "I'll take Janet with me. I've got to start riding the new horse tomorrow. You should see him. He's absolutely gorgeous."

Her mother said, "It wouldn't hurt you to do something besides going to the barnyard every day."

"Yes, it would," said Middie. "I have to ride lots. I want to win the Junior Jumping Championship at Idlewood some day."

"You'll never win anything," said Laurie, "because you never really work hard at it. Like your painting. You don't even finish half the pictures you start."

Middie hunched her shoulders.

She pretended not to see her mother and father

exchange glances, and she lapsed into silence.

She wondered what Janet would think of the new horse. Middie had met Janet only last week, but she thought Janet was a little strange. She bragged a lot about her horse, Silver Minaret, who was back in Connecticut, but not once did she ask Middie if there was someplace they could go riding together. Middie was sure she could talk Janet into going to Mrs. Bailey's, but she wasn't planning to let Janet ride the new horse. Even if Janet begged her to, which wasn't likely. Middie wasn't going to let anyone else ride that horse.

In a trance, Middie sat through the rest of dinner, imagining herself in the big arena at Idlewood, galloping the glorious creature that even now was waiting for her at Mrs. Bailey's. If only she could enter him in a show, she knew without a doubt that she could win some ribbons with him. Maybe she could even win a silver trophy.

5.
Janet

Middie got up early the next morning and finished two of her stable jobs before she went next door to David's. Janet was wandering around the backyard by herself, looking at the garden. Her deep brown eyes brightened when she saw Middie.

"Nice outfit," said Middie, noticing Janet's bright red shorts and cotton shirt with red horses printed all over it. She even had red socks and white tennis shoes, and a red ribbon in her hair. "It's cute."

"Hey, I'm glad we're going to the beach today," said Janet. "I'm all ready."

"I wanted to talk to you about that," Middie said. "There's a new horse at Mrs. Bailey's that I can ride like he's my own, and I want you to go with me to see him. I'm going to start riding him today."

"Oh." Janet bent over and examined a flower. "You sure have a lot of flowers here I've never seen before. My mother would go bananas."

"We've got those, too," said Middie. "There's a banana tree in our backyard."

Janet smiled faintly. "Well, I did sort of want to go to the beach today. I don't feel like riding."

"I didn't mean for you to ride. I meant just to look at him and tell me what you think of him."

"Oh." She straightened up. "I guess I could."

"Come on, Janet. This horse is a jumper, and don't you know a lot about jumping?"

Janet brightened. "Oh, yes! My horse is a fantastic jumper. We've won a lot of ribbons."

"How super!" said Middie. She wished she didn't feel as though an arrow had gone right through her middle. "This is only your first week — we've got all summer to go to the beach. Let's go to Mrs. Bailey's, and you can tell her all about your horse."

Janet shrugged. "Well, okay. David's letting me use his ten-speed." She twisted a lock of hair around one finger. "Is it very far to Mrs. Bailey's?"

"Not far. First stop is the Kellers'. I muck out their stables and feed their horses. If you help, we can get through twice as fast."

"I guess I can help if you'll show me what to do."

Middie hunted up Laurie. "You and David can be as mushy as you want to at the beach. We're going to Mrs. Bailey's."

"Sometimes," said Laurie, "you show signs of

having a brain. I don't know how you did it, but that's great."

Middie and Janet pedaled through the tree-lined streets with the morning sun already hot on their backs.

"Tell me again about your horse," said Middie.

"He's a conformation hunter. He's a thorough-bred, gray, sixteen hands, twelve years old." She recited it carefully. "His show name is Silver Min-aret, and we call him Minaret. He's won lots of ribbons and trophies in the 'A' circuit." She smiled at Middie. "Tell me about your new horse."

"I don't know much about him except that he used to be a racehorse, and he's a jumper now."

"You must be awfully good if your trainer has you ride horses like that."

Middie shrugged. "Mrs. Bailey wants me to ride different kinds of horses. I'm lucky to have her for my trainer because she's really good. It's partly a trade-off for taking care of her horse. I used to take lessons at the Riding Club, but I had to stop when my brother went away to college."

"Your brother must be a pain."

They pedaled in silence for a minute. Middie didn't want to tell her that Keith had wanted to go to a special college back East, but with Middie in the family it was too expensive. He'd had to settle for the State University. Middie sighed. "Keith isn't a pain. He's okay."

And Laurie couldn't even go to State — she

31

would be starting junior college right in their own hometown. There were lots of other plans Middie had messed up, too. No wonder her brother and sisters hadn't wanted her.

"My trainer is super," said Janet. "What's Mrs. Bailey like?"

"She's fantastic. She used to ride the Grand Prix jumping circuit. You should see her trophies and ribbons, and the scrapbooks with all her pictures. She fixes it so she can give me lessons on different people's horses, and she's a great teacher, even if she can't ride anymore."

"How come she can't ride?"

Middie pedaled more slowly. "She had a bad accident a long time ago. Her horse rolled down the mountainside with her."

Janet shuddered. "What happened to the horse?"

"That's Derry," Middie said cheerfully. "He's in her backyard. He's not sound enough to ride, but he's not in pain. She just keeps him for company."

"It would be funny having somebody teach you who couldn't ride."

"Mrs. Bailey isn't a bit funny; she's great. Wait till you meet her." Middie pointed. "There's the Kellers' house."

They stopped at a big yellow-and-white barn behind an attractive yellow house with white trim. Middie showed Janet where the hay was, and how much to feed, while she raked out the stalls and put in fresh shavings.

"How can you stand cleaning up after horses?" asked Janet as they pedaled through the streets again. "And they're not even yours. Thank heavens my horse is at a stable, and somebody else does that."

"I kind of like mucking out stalls," declared Middie. "It's cleaning up my room that I hate. And how can you stand being without your horse all summer?"

Janet shrugged. "I don't mind. My trainer is having another girl ride him on the show circuit. My mom is paying all the entry fees so I get to keep the ribbons. I'll have just as many as if I'd stayed home and ridden him."

Middie was silent. "I didn't know you could do that," she finally said. But what good were ribbons if you didn't earn them yourself? Middie wondered. "What does your mom think about that?"

Janet pedaled away for a minute without saying anything. "Actually, it was Mom's idea, since I wanted to come out here for the summer. She didn't want me to lose out on any ribbons."

"But you're not winning them, really."

"I know. Tell that to my mom." Janet's voice wavered.

"Oh," said Middie. She wished she hadn't said anything. "At least it's your horse that's winning."

Janet smiled uncertainly. "Yeah."

"Well, I'm glad you came to California. My best friend, B. J., took her horse and went to riding camp for the summer. It's too expensive for me to go, so I haven't had anybody to pal around with till you came."

Janet flashed her a smile, and Middie smiled back.

"Last stop is the Jamisons'," said Middie after a while. "I have to pick up my helmet there. I ride Mrs. Jamison's horse Peaches three times a week."

"Why doesn't Mrs. Jamison ride her?"

"She does, but not as much as she wants to because she works. I'm sort of training Peaches for her because she says the mare is scary. She takes lessons from Joshua Logan on Saturdays."

"Why doesn't that Joshua Logan train Peaches?"

"Mrs. Jamison wants her horse here at home where she can take care of her."

"Even though she's scared of her? Why doesn't she sell Peaches and get a horse she's not scared of?"

Middie grinned. "She loves Peaches. She won't ever sell her. Here we are."

The palomino was hanging her golden head over the pasture fence. She nickered when she saw Middie.

"Oh, she *is* beautiful," said Janet. "No wonder Mrs. Jamison loves her."

Middie laughed. Janet stood outside the fence

and carefully patted the palomino while Middie went in the barn and brought out her helmet. "Now I'm ready for the new horse!" She buckled it on the handlebars, and the two girls whizzed off down the street.

Mrs. Bailey was waiting on the front porch, her hunting saddle laid out on the railing.

"This is Janet, and she's staying at David Willoughby's for the summer, and she has a conformation hunter named Silver Minaret," announced Middie.

"Conformation hunter!" said Mrs. Bailey. "How nice!"

Janet tucked her hair in back of her ears. "He's a super jumper. I've won a lot of classes with him, and I've had him only a year. He jumps five feet."

Again, Middie felt that arrow in her middle.

"My, that sounds exciting," said Mrs. Bailey. "Do you have any pictures of him?"

"I have loads of pictures, but I didn't bring any. They're all back in Connecticut."

"That's too bad," said Mrs. Bailey. "Well, come and tell me all about this wonderful horse of yours while Middie gets her horse ready."

Middie bit her lip and turned to go to the barn.

6.
Happy Holiday

The big chestnut stood tense and stiff as Middie began grooming him. She used the dandy brush slowly, carefully, then the curry and the body brush, all over his upper body, talking to him as she worked.

Middie took longer brushing him than she wanted to, but she could tell that he liked it. Under the steady rhythm of the brush the tenseness went out of his muscles, and his breathing became slow and even.

While she was brushing the big horse she discovered a number of scars. The worst was a huge jagged one that ran from his shoulder and chest partway down his left foreleg.

"That must have been a terrible accident," she said, carefully tracing the outline of the scar with one finger. "If only you could talk and tell me about it. You must have crashed into something that really sliced you open. It's a wonder they didn't put you down." She studied the scar and shuddered. Then she leaned over and gently kissed it. She looked up at him and smiled. "But it doesn't keep you from being awfully handsome." The horse took a deep breath and let it out in a long slow sigh.

Middie cleaned his hooves and stood back to look at him. He had been clipped and trimmed for the auction, and in spite of his being so thin, his coat shone. Middie sighed with happiness. She didn't care if Janet's horse could jump *ten* feet. She went into the tack room and brought out the horse's bridle.

Mrs. Bailey settled herself on the bench at the edge of the field with Janet beside her. Middie hung the bridle on the fence and picked up the pad and hunting saddle.

"Aren't you going to put on your boots and breeches?"

Middie shook her head. "I save them for shows. I'd rather wear jeans."

"My trainer always makes us ride in boots and breeches."

"What a pain," said Middie. She had only rubber boots, which were hot and sticky in summer and cold and clammy in winter. She desperately wanted leather boots, but there wasn't a chance. Somehow there were always school clothes that had to be bought instead.

She took three steps toward the big horse.

The thoroughbred stiffened in alarm and showed the whites of his eyes.

"Easy, boy, easy," Middie said, carefully lifting

the saddle onto his back. He stepped around nervously but she managed to buckle the girth anyway. When she went to bridle him, he jerked his head away.

Janet said quickly, "I don't think this is a good horse for you to ride."

Middie grabbed the horse's nose and held it firmly till she got the bridle on. The horse broke into a sweat and swung back and forth.

"What's the matter with you?" Middie asked the horse. She tried to pat him, but he sidestepped. "I'm not going to hurt you. Promise." She said to Mrs. Bailey, "I think I'd better exercise him on the lunge line before I mount him."

Mrs. Bailey nodded. "You know where the lunge line is."

Middie led the thoroughbred into the field used as an arena and fixed his bridle so the reins couldn't slip over his head. She ran one end of the cotton lunge line through the bridle and snapped it onto the bit. She gathered the other end in her left hand and stood back so she could make the horse work in a circle around her.

"Walk," she said firmly.

He started to trot in a circle around her, then swung to face her and stopped. She popped the lunge whip at him.

"Walk!" she commanded. He started to trot, swung to face her, and stopped.

Middie couldn't move fast enough to get behind him. He would trot a few strides, swing, and stop, ears alert and eyes fixed on her face.

No matter what command she gave him, he didn't seem to understand. He began breathing quickly and he started to shake.

"He's getting really nervous," said Middie. She turned to Janet. "Here, you hold the whip and lunge line while I ride him. Then he'll have to obey me."

Janet shook her head quickly. "Oh, no, I can't do that. I've *never* used a lunge line, and I'm not going to start now. Don't ask me to." She began twisting a lock of her hair. "This isn't a good horse for you."

"That's not so," protested Middie, turning to Mrs. Bailey. "What am I doing wrong?"

The crinkled face was puzzled. "Something does seem to be wrong, but I don't think it's your fault." She smiled at Middie. "You're a fair enough rider; mount up and see what you can do."

Janet objected, "She'll get hurt."

"No, I won't," said Middie, hoping she wouldn't. Janet sure wasn't helping. The horse danced around, but Middie sprang into the saddle before he could get away from her. She stroked the copper neck and tried to calm him.

The horse pranced and jigged, first one way and then the other. Middie decided it was safer to push him into a trot. The chestnut shot forward so quickly, he almost left Middie behind. She bounced uncomfortably. That was enough for the horse. He threw his head up and bolted.

Janet screamed. Middie struggled with the horse and finally spun him in a tight circle. They halted.

"Listen, fella," said Middie, gasping, "you're not to gallop until I tell you to." She glanced over her shoulder. Janet looked scared and white, but the old lady was smiling.

"Good," said Mrs. Bailey. "Keep going. He needs work, and lots of it."

"Then that's what he'll get," said Middie. She was proud of the way she had handled the horse. Janet might win ribbons, but Middie would show her a thing or two about riding.

The thoroughbred quivered and tossed his head up and down. Middie pushed him into the trot again. This time she was ready for it, and he swung into a mile-consuming gait that made her feel like she was floating. She was enjoying it so much, she forgot to watch where she was going. She suddenly saw the fence at the edge of the field directly in front of her. She pulled hard to swing around the corner.

The horse didn't like being jerked. He spun and bolted, peeling Middie neatly off the saddle. She crashed into the fence and lay still. The thoroughbred, his stirrups flying, raced on around the field as though he had just burst from the starting gate.

Middie rolled over and sat up in time to watch the thoroughbred round the field at the far end.

She felt hypnotized. The sheer beauty of the galloping horse made her throat ache.

"I'll get back on," she whispered. "You're not going to scare me off. I'm going to ride you."

"Are you hurt?" yelled Janet, her face pale, running toward Middie.

Middie grinned and stood up. "Nope, not this time. He's kind of neat, isn't he?"

Janet stopped in her tracks. "Meredith Scott, you almost gave me a heart attack when he threw you like that."

"Sorry about that," said Middie, brushing off her jeans. "Help me catch him, will you?"

Janet shook her head quickly. "No way! That horse scares me." She stepped back and suddenly waved her arms as he went careening by.

"Not like that!" said Middie. Didn't Janet know *anything* about horses? "Let's walk into the center and stand quietly until he slows down."

Janet shook her head. "I don't feel so good. I'm going to go sit down."

The thoroughbred slowed to a walk and finally began to graze. He lifted his head as Middie approached, but he stood still. Middie picked up his reins and patted him.

"Whew," said Middie. "Maybe he'll be quieter now that he's had a chance to gallop some more."

"That horse is a holy terror, and you're going to get hurt," declared Janet. "You'd better put him back in the barn."

What a dumb thing to say, thought Middie. She glanced at Mrs. Bailey. The old lady smiled and nodded to her, so Middie gathered up the reins.

The horse was less nervous when she mounted him the second time. She concentrated on giving the commands more gently, and asked him alternately to walk and trot around the field. Little by little, she felt him soften and listen to her. His trot stride was enormous. She began to enjoy herself.

Middie signaled him to canter, and he struck off smoothly. Any fear of being run away with vanished in awe as she felt his rhythm and power. She leaned forward and let him gallop on.

The chestnut began to snort happily with each stride. Middie grinned and she stroked his neck as they flew.

"You know what I think?" Middie asked the horse as they cut across one corner of the field. "Riding you is like having a super vacation — better than going away on a trip. You're like a holiday."

A minute later she laughed. "That's what I'll call you till I find out your real name. You're my Happy Holiday."

Even after his long gallop, the horse didn't want to walk; he danced.

"Patience, patience," called out Mrs. Bailey.

"Isn't he stupendous?" Middie asked.

"Just what I suspected," said Mrs. Bailey. Her

eyes were sparkling. "I knew it the moment I laid eyes on him."

Janet added, "My trainer says horses like that are never dependable. Sooner or later, Middie will get hurt. She ought to have a reliable horse instead."

"He's not hard to ride!" exclaimed Middie. "He pulls quite a bit, but steadily. I think he's used to somebody big and strong riding him."

"He might have been a man's horse," Mrs. Bailey said. "I think he's had quite a bit of training. It will be a challenge to see how much of it you can bring back. He must have been impressive when he was young."

"He can't be *very* old," said Middie. "You saw him run! But he's terribly thin. Couldn't we give him some A and M?"

"What's that?" asked Janet.

"Alfalfa chopped up with molasses," said Mrs. Bailey. "I ordered a couple of sacks yesterday; it should be here this afternoon. I'll have the feed man put an empty barrel in the stall, and pour the A and M into that."

"He'll love it." Middie's face grew pink, and she smiled. "I've thought of what I can call him till we find out his real name — Happy Holiday! Is that okay?"

"Very good!" The white head nodded vigorously. "Now trot him around the field one more time, and this time don't let him cut those corners."

"Okay," said Middie. Again she felt the swinging, mile-crossing gait. She guided him firmly for the corner. He pricked his ears and collected himself. Middie did not realize what was happening in time to prevent it.

7.
A Big Mistake

The thoroughbred took one powerful canter stride and leaped for the top of the five-foot fence. Middie shot forward from the saddle. She landed on his neck, grabbed his mane, and hung on. The horse skimmed over the fence and galloped up the hill, while Middie clutched at anything she could to stay with him. When they reached the top of the hill and he put his head up, she half slid and half scrambled back into the saddle and halted him. He jigged sideways, snorting loudly.

When the horse had suddenly seen the five-foot fence in front of him, he had gathered and launched himself into space. It was just like the time the gooseneck rail of the racetrack had unexpectedly appeared before him when he was bumped hard by another horse. He had felt the saddle lighten as he went over the fence, but this rider was hanging on as he galloped up the hill. He remembered people screaming and running as he had galloped through the crowd, jumping benches and tables and everything in his way. Then there had been a sharp raw pain in his left foreleg, and he'd had to stop. They had taken him away from the track in a big trailer, and he had never raced again.

He started to tremble, but the girl leaned forward and threw her arms around his neck. The horse tossed his head.

"You are fantastic!" exclaimed Middie. "Holiday, I love you."

She suddenly remembered the others. She turned and rode back down to meet them as they were hurrying up the hill, Mrs. Bailey's cane scattering the stones.

"Stayed on him, I see," said Mrs. Bailey sharply.

"Did you see him?" shouted Middie. "Did you see that?"

"How could I miss it?" said Mrs. Bailey. "I asked you to go deep in the corner, not over the top of it."

Janet collapsed onto a tree stump and said, "Omigosh!"

Middie giggled. "I'm sorry, Mrs. Bailey. I've never jumped that high before. I know I was awful, but wasn't he just great?"

"He is certainly athletic, and he's apparently had a lot of training." Mrs. Bailey's face was stern. "That means much more work for you. And none

46

of your famous timesaving shortcuts, either."

"Okay," said Middie, grinning.

"Now take him back into the field and ride him into that corner properly. There's no excuse for letting a horse jump a fence you didn't intend to take."

"Okay," said Middie, still grinning.

Middie practiced riding into the corners until Mrs. Bailey was satisfied. She slid off and began leading the horse to cool him out. "You're going back to school," she told him. "You're going to remember everything you used to know."

Janet fell into step beside her. "Your horse sure can jump. He's almost as good as Minaret."

"Almost! What do you mean?"

"Well, Minaret would never take a fence unless I told him to."

"He thought I did tell him." Middie glared at her. "I just don't know all his cues yet."

"My trainer wouldn't like that horse at all. You should have your mother get you a really good horse that does exactly what you want. Then you can jump everything and win all the ribbons you want."

"Forget it!" said Middie. "My mother will *never* buy me a horse — they're too expensive. Dad doesn't even *like* horses. If I want a horse, I'll have to buy him myself."

"I guess I'm lucky," said Janet. "My mom loves horses and horse shows. She and my trainer figure out which shows I should enter so I can win the most ribbons. Mom gets mad at the judge when I don't win."

"No wonder you've got a good horse." She could feel the excitement of jumping the big fence begin to fade.

"Mom pays a groom to wash and braid my horse and tack him up and everything," Janet went on. "She helps me get ready."

"That's great," said Middie without conviction.

"Too bad your mother isn't like mine," said Janet.

"It wouldn't do me any good," said Middie. "We couldn't afford that anyway."

"Oh," said Janet. "I really *am* lucky."

Middie sighed. "Come on while I put Holiday away."

Middie led Holiday back to the barn and tied him to the tie rail. It wasn't fair for Janet to have everything, thought Middie. Janet didn't mind being without her horse all summer. Sometimes she acted as though she didn't know *anything* about horses — she didn't even know how to catch a loose horse! And was Janet ever scared of Holiday! Middie looked up at the big chestnut horse and felt more cheerful.

Janet began twisting a lock of hair around one finger. "I wish I could help, but there isn't anything I can do."

"Sure there is. When I start jumping him, you can help set up the jumps."

"I'd like that. As long as you don't ask me to do anything with that horse."

Middie smiled. "I won't."

A bell began clanging loudly on the front porch.

"What's that?" exclaimed Janet.

"That means the telephone is ringing."

"I'll get it," said Janet. She dashed off, leaving Mrs. Bailey to follow.

Middie had just put Holiday in his stall when Janet called to her. "Middie, Mrs. Bailey wants you to answer the kitchen phone. She says it's Halsey, the horse trainer. He wants to tell you about that horse."

Middie shot up the stairs, eager to ask Halsey a hundred questions.

Halsey sounded amused. "Sure I can tell you all about that old horse. His name is Rusty. Came from a riding stable. The owner died, and the wife sold out and shipped 'bout thirty head of saddle horses to the Pomona auction. That's where I picked him up."

Middie asked, "Was he a great show horse once? How old is he?"

Halsey laughed. "He's a good looker, ain't he? Guess he was a show horse once — long ago must have been a good jumper. He don't look his age — in his twenties, I figger."

"*That* old?" exclaimed Middie. "He sure doesn't act like it."

"Fella at the auction said he was a fav'rit for

49

beginners. I got him for my ten-year-old grandson to learn to ride on."

"To learn to ride on?" echoed Middie, stupefied.

Mrs. Bailey interrupted. "Your grandson doesn't know how to ride at all?"

"No, ma'am," said Halsey. "He's been on some trail rides just sittin', but it's time he started learnin' what to do when he's on board."

Mrs. Bailey cleared her throat. "Halsey, you'd better come and watch Middie ride this horse. I think there's been a big mistake."

"Oh, yeah?" said Halsey. "I ain't picked a good horse?"

"You certainly picked a good one, but not for anyone to learn to ride on. You'll have to come and see him in action."

They hung up, and Middie raced into the living room. "Somebody's crazy!" she exclaimed. "That's no horse for a beginner!"

"You're absolutely right!" A frown crossed Mrs. Bailey's face. "I suppose there was a school horse named Rusty, but Holiday certainly doesn't fit that description."

"What should I do?" asked Middie.

"Keep on riding him, and call him Happy Holiday. It's up to Halsey to find out who he is, if he can. He'll have to decide what to do next."

"That's okay by me." She went to the window and stared down at the barn. Holiday had put his head out of the stall door and was looking off into the distance again. Even from there she could see the beautiful head with its unusual star, a kite with a curly tail. And he was hers to ride for . . . well, who knew? Maybe, just *maybe*, she'd be able to enter him in some jumping shows before Halsey took him away.

She shivered a little. That is no kid's horse, she said to herself. He must have been really great when he was young; he's still terrific. Maybe he was famous. How in the world did he end up at the Pomona auction?

She remembered the surge of power as they had neared the corner of the field, and then the incredible lift-off to the top of the fence, so effortless and accurate in spite of her not expecting it. If ever she had a chance to win at Idlewood, Holiday was the horse!

Middie turned to Mrs. Bailey. "I can hardly wait to start jumping him. Jan will help me set up the jumps. Can you give me a lesson tomorrow?"

"Certainly, but it will be quite a while before you start jumping. You will have to take your time with exercises to make him flexible. And you need to learn how to control him."

"He already knows how to jump, and I *can* control him," protested Middie. "Didn't you see me stop him when he was running away?"

"You shouldn't have let him get started. And jumping well consistently is quite different from going over a fence by accident."

Middie scowled. "He thought I wanted him to."

"Balderdash! You did not ask him to jump!"

Mrs. Bailey looked stern. "You can begin re-schooling him, but you must go slowly. No short-cuts and no rushing through. We have no way of knowing what experiences he's had." The old lady straightened up and looked hard at Middie. "One thing I'm sure of — you've never ridden a horse with that much talent. It's going to be a real challenge to bring out the best in him."

8.
The Discovery

Middie could hardly sleep that night for thinking of her first lesson on Holiday. To ride a horse who could jump like that! Maybe Idlewood wasn't just a dream.

The A and M had been delivered, and the big horse had his head out of sight in the barrel when Middie, halter in hand, went into his stall. "Hey, big fella," she said cheerfully, "it's time for a real lesson." She gave him a friendly pat on his rump as she walked by. The horse leapt up and whirled to face her, his eyes wide with alarm.

Middie jumped out of his way and stared. As soon as Holiday saw who it was, he relaxed and nickered.

"You didn't hear me!" exclaimed Middie.

Holiday stepped forward and rubbed his muzzle against her shirt. She didn't even notice the green smear.

Middie shivered. "I was talking to you, but you didn't know I was here until I touched you!"

Holiday went back to the A and M. She clapped

her hands and said in a very loud voice, "Hey, Holiday! Back up!"

He kept on eating.

Middie drew in her breath sharply. "You can't hear anything. You really . . . are . . . deaf." She felt as though a stone had landed in her stomach. "That's why you wouldn't work on the lunge line. You couldn't hear my commands."

Holiday lifted his head and chewed while he watched her. She thought, he lives and moves in a world forever silent. He can't hear the wind in the trees, or the meadowlarks warble from the fence posts. He won't hear me sing to him out on the trail.

She swallowed hard. She had to face the facts. A horse that couldn't hear voice commands was risky. Maybe even dangerous. Tears welled up in her eyes.

What would Mrs. Bailey do when she found out? She might not let Middie ride him anymore. And her parents — for sure they wouldn't. Halsey would take him away. She wouldn't ever be able to enter him in a show.

"Oh, Holiday," she said and put her arms around his neck, her cheek against the shining coat. Her thoughts and feelings were in a muddle. She leaned against him, and some of the horse's strength seemed to flow into her own body. Slowly she sorted out her thoughts.

Holiday turned and nudged her as though to ask what was the matter. She wiped the tears from her face and straightened up, one idea firm in her mind. She said very quietly, "I'm not going to tell anybody you're deaf. I'll ride you just like before, and nobody's going to know."

She smiled bravely. "I'll just have to be careful you can see me before I touch you. I'll talk to you and treat you as though you *do* hear everything. We'll learn to understand each other so well, it won't matter if you can't hear." She hugged him again. "It's going to be okay."

She fastened his halter and led him to the tie rail, smiling and talking to him as though nothing had happened. While she groomed him and tacked him up, she thought hard. He was so well-trained, he couldn't have been deaf for very long. Maybe the big scar on his chest and leg had something to do with his being deaf. Maybe when he crashed into whatever it was, he had hit his head. It would take a while for somebody to figure out he couldn't hear. She thought, I'll bet that's why he got to the auction with the name of Rusty.

After that, Middie didn't have time to think about his past. She had never worked so hard. She had all her stables to do twice a day, she rode Peaches three times a week, and now she had to ride Holiday every morning for an hour.

Circle twice on the short side of the field, three or four times on the long side.

Janet, in purple shorts and a lavender T-shirt and a purple ribbon in her hair, sat under the oak tree eating an orange, watching Middie ride.

Derry trotted in a limp up and down in his paddock, snorting and glaring at the thoroughbred who was getting all the attention.

Circle, circle, spiral, circle.

"Don't you think he's getting tired?" asked Middie, wiping the sweat from her face as they trotted briskly by.

Mrs. Bailey made a sound of derision. "Not *that* horse." She looked at Middie's face. "But you can take a break if you want to."

Middie breathed a sigh of relief and loosened the reins. Up went the horse's head, and off he galloped.

Middie scrambled wildly for the reins. Half a minute later she pulled him in a tight circle and brought him to a halt. She caught her breath while Holiday snorted happily. She looked over her shoulder at Mrs. Bailey.

The old lady was smiling.

"Oh, all right," said Middie under her breath. Circle walk, circle trot, spiral, reverse, circle some more.

Toward the end of the fourth week, the horse wasn't arguing with Middie as often. She could feel he was better at bending on the circle, and his transitions from one gait to another were smoother.

"Not bad. Not bad at all," said Mrs. Bailey as Middie rounded the corner at a sparkling trot, feet out of the stirrups and legs glued to his side. "He's beginning to look like a horse instead of a giraffe. He's come a long way in less than a month."

"I guess I'm teaching him a lot," said Middie, looking hopefully at Mrs. Bailey.

"You're not teaching him anything new; you're refreshing his memory. Someone gave that horse years of careful training, and he didn't use any shortcuts. That horse has been teaching *you*."

Middie felt her face turn pink. She halted abruptly in front of Janet.

Janet backed away hastily. "Not so close!"

"He won't hurt you," said Middie. She dropped the reins carelessly on his neck.

"Well, I don't trust him. You can't trust horses."

"Don't you trust Minaret?"

"That's different," Janet said. "Sure, I do. But he's awfully well-trained. Did I tell you we won the Junior Championship at the Westchester Show this spring?"

"Not that one," said Middie. "You told me about a lot of other shows."

"Here, have a piece of my orange." She gave a little shriek as the horse swung around. "Don't get so CLOSE."

Middie popped the orange into her mouth and bit down. Cold juice squirted pleasantly over her tongue. "That is *good*."

Janet pulled off another section and offered it. "The Westchester Show is one of the biggest shows where I come from. The fences for the last round were set at four feet with great big spreads."

Middie swallowed. "And you and Minaret jumped those?" She couldn't imagine Janet riding a big hunter, let alone one jumping four-foot fences.

"Sure we did," said Janet, concentrating on the orange. "Minaret just loves to jump." She handed Middie another piece.

Middie chewed slowly. You certainly couldn't judge people by appearances. "I wish I could win something like that," she said. "I wish I could show Laurie that she isn't the only one who can win trophies."

"I thought Laurie played tennis."

"She does. And every time she wins a tournament or something, Mom and Dad make a big fuss over her."

"But how can you win anything when you don't have a horse you can show?" asked Janet.

"Exactly!" said Middie. "They think Laurie is so great. If only I could win in horse shows, they'd begin to make a fuss over *me*."

Janet rolled her eyes. "I'm glad I don't have a sister."

There was a little silence. Mrs. Bailey spoke. "Middie, you and Holiday have been working hard for almost a month. How about taking him out on the trail for a change? He hasn't tried to bolt for some time."

"You mean ride him up the canyon?" Middie asked.

The old lady nodded. "Don't canter — just walk. You might be able to trot a little, with caution. Janet can keep an eye on you from the gate and tell me how he goes."

Middie started to say, "What good would that do?" but Mrs. Bailey's eyes were steely gray. "Come on, Jan," she said. "Down by the gate there's a big oak tree that's easy to climb. You can see almost the whole canyon from there."

As they neared the gate, Holiday snorted at the clumps of sagebrush beyond, and he began to dance and jig sideways, first one way and then the other. Middie shortened her reins and tried to keep a steady contact.

The smell of the sagebrush and chaparral, the sight of the rolling hills and canyon, brought memories flooding back to Holiday and the excitement of being turned out for the first time in the mountains. He had been shut up in a stall with a cast on his foreleg for such a long time that sometimes he had tried to kick the stall apart. And then there was a long trailer trip, and when he was led down the ramp he saw barns and corrals at the foot of tall mountains, and beyond the corrals he couldn't see any fences at all.

"Easy, boy, easy," said Middie, stroking his neck with one hand while holding the reins and his mane in the other. He tossed his head up and down and snorted loudly.

"Holiday's too excited," said Janet. "Maybe you shouldn't take him out yet. Let's just walk around and go back to the barn."

"Oh, no. It's probably been a long time since he was out on a trail. It'll be good for him — I bet he loves it."

Janet's hand hesitated on the gate latch. "Are you sure he won't throw you?"

"Sure, I'm sure," said Middie, feeling very unsure. Holiday was leaping around more and more, trying to break away. "He'll be okay once we get started," she said, hoping it was true.

Janet opened the gate and stood back. Holiday plunged through while Middie struggled to keep him in hand. He threw his head up and half-trotted, half-cantered into the canyon.

For Holiday, it was almost like that first time he had been turned out to pasture in the mountains without even a halter. His leg still hurt some and he had to favor it, but he had nearly gone wild with the freedom. He remembered finding a band of horses to run with in the mountains and after a while, he could run and jump better than he ever had before.

Middie guided the bounding horse onto the trail where the canyon was wide and almost flat. A single stream had carved the canyon from the mountains. In winter, the stream was a torrent that swept a tangle of windfallen trees and huge gray boulders before it, but in summer it shrank to a meandering little brook that finally disappeared into the sandy streambed. Hikers and horses had worn paths on both sides.

It was impossible to make Holiday walk. He jumped up and down, cantered a few strides in place, and almost jerked the reins from her hands.

Maybe he'll be easier to handle if I let him gallop first, she thought. Mrs. Bailey doesn't think I can manage him, but I bet I can.

After a turn in the trail she gave him the canter signal. Off they flew at a full gallop, Holiday blowing loudly at every stride.

The big horse's speed and determination frightened Middie. The banks on either side became a blur; the wind was sharp against her face. She glimpsed a huge log that had fallen across the trail; they skimmed it. A large pile of driftwood was next. It looked formidable, but they jumped it while Middie was thinking they ought to go around it. Landslides, mounds of rocks, windfallen trees rushed at her; Holiday took them all without breaking stride. Holiday's hooves rang over the hard-packed trail as he and the girl galloped up the canyon, his nostrils flaring with excitement.

The trail curved around the cliff and forded the stream. Holiday swung around the curve, jumped the entire brook, and galloped on up the other side.

Middie suddenly realized that in spite of his headlong rush, he was studying the ground carefully. He was measuring his own approach to each obstacle and jumping in stride.

The fear drained out of her. He knows what he's doing, she thought with a kind of wonder. He's not running away; he's racing and jumping! He thinks that's what I want!

She laughed and patted his neck as they galloped.

The trail ascended a steep bank. Holiday leaped to the top, took two strides, and plunged down on the other side. Middie shouted with glee and began looking for a place to slow down. They had galloped far enough.

Now Middie could see a little gully ahead, widened by erosion to form a small ravine. They had already jumped some streams and banks that were wider.

"This is the last jump," Middie told him.

Holiday had been galloping across country just as he used to do with the boy called Brian on his back, and every obstacle was exciting to jump. And then suddenly there was the gully, reminding him of the ravine that once had yawned in front of him in the desert. He had tried to jump the ravine, but something had gone wrong. The memory of the shock and the pain that followed flooded his body and terrified him. He spun away hard to the right.

Middle was so confident that Holiday would take the jump that when he abruptly stiffened and swerved from the ravine, it took her completely by surprise. She shot out of the saddle and hit the dirt.

9.
From Despair to Delight

Middie landed flat on her back. She couldn't move; her lungs felt as though they were on fire. She wanted to take a breath, and could not.

You're going to be okay, she tried to tell herself. You just had the wind knocked out of you.

She couldn't yell for help, even if she wanted to. What if she couldn't ever take another breath?

The burning in her chest stopped suddenly, and sweet air rushed into her lungs. She took a long shuddering breath. And another. She was breathing again.

What in the world had happened? She closed her eyes to concentrate. She had to think, to try to remember.

Now she knew. Holiday had refused the ravine. But why? And where was he? She sat up and looked around.

Fifty yards away stood the thoroughbred, covered with lather. His head was down, and one foreleg was caught in the reins trailing on the ground.

Middie slowly stood up, took a deep breath, and walked toward him. He lifted his head slightly as she approached.

She reached out one hand and touched him. "Poor boy," she said softly, running her fingers in small circles up his neck. He was trembling and breathing hard. "Easy, boy, easy."

Middie heard running footsteps. Around the corner of the trail came Janet, her face white and worried.

"Thank heavens you're all right!" she panted. "I saw him run away with you and I was sure you'd be killed!"

"Not yet," said Middie. "He didn't run away with me; he just refused that little ditch. I want to untangle his reins before he breaks them."

"Who cares about reins? Come on, I'll walk home with you. He can go back to the barn by himself."

Middie stared at her. "With a saddle and bridle on? You're crazy." What did Janet think, anyway?

Janet shook her head.

Middie groaned. "Okay, at least wait until I fix his bridle."

The horse let her pick up his foreleg and free the reins. "Look how he's shaking!" she exclaimed, astonished. "He's still scared to death!"

"He'd better be scared. He was a bad horse, and he knows he's going to be whipped."

"If that's so, he would have run away from me, but he didn't. He's scared, but not of being whipped."

Janet stepped back. "Aren't you going to punish him for refusing?"

Middie put her arms around his neck and stroked him gently. "He didn't mean to stop. Something about that gully frightened him."

Janet walked over to the gully and peered down. "There's absolutely nothing down there. You'd better whip him."

Middie exploded. "You don't know *anything* about horses. Whipping never cures being scared."

"Let's go back to the barn, right now."

Middie thought a minute. "Maybe he got hurt at a ditch, and that's why he refused." She gathered up the reins.

"What are you going to do now?" Janet's eyes were big.

"I'm going to jump that little ditch. I'll walk him around first till he calms down, and then we'll jump it." She swung up into the saddle.

Janet put her hands to her face. "He won't. Please, let's go home."

"He will. I can't let him get away with this. He's jumped things wider than that ditch."

Janet sat down on a rock with her head cradled in her arms. Middie heard her say, "I feel sick to my stomach," but Middie was too intent on Holiday to pay attention.

When Middie felt the horse was calm again, she trotted to the ravine, her jaw set. She drove him with her legs and before takeoff smacked him once with the crop. At the last second he swerved as sharply as before. Middie grabbed his mane and hung on.

"That was close," Middie panted. She smacked him quickly twice more and turned him again toward the ravine.

Janet looked up. "Okay, you've tried enough," she said. "Now let's go home. When somebody gets hurt, I throw up."

"I won't get hurt. I've got to make him jump it."

But she couldn't. She couldn't even walk him up to look at it. He stopped or spun away. He began shaking again, and sweat broke out over his body. It darkened his flanks and ran down his belly.

Middie was close to tears. "I'm just not good enough. A really good rider could make him go over." She looked at Janet. "You've jumped more than I have. What am I doing wrong?"

Janet shook her head. "My trainer would never let me get near a horse like that. We've got to go back to the barn."

Middie bit her lip in frustration. Janet wasn't any help at all!

Silently they walked all the way home. By the time they reached the gate, Holiday was no longer shaking, and his coat was nearly dry.

When Middie untacked him, he reached around

and shoved his nose against her shirt. She gave him a piece of carrot and he munched happily as though nothing had happened.

She sighed. "I know you're sorry." She would ask Mrs. Bailey what to do to make Holiday jump that ravine. She wasn't going to give up.

Janet glanced up at the porch. "There's an old man with Mrs. Bailey. She's waving for us to come up."

"Why, it's Halsey!" Middie swallowed hard. What if he had come to take the horse away?

Halsey clumped down the steps in his heavy boots and pushed his broad-brimmed hat to the back of his head. He was short and stocky, with white hair and deep blue eyes in a face like wrinkled leather.

"You put on quite a show," he said. "We was watchin' from the porch and saw some of your wild ride. You okay?"

"Oh, sure. He's a fantastic jumper, isn't he? Except for that gully."

"Oh, yeah. One thing I know, that sure ain't no kid's horse. You done well to ride him. But Mizz Bailey's real mad at you for galloping him when she said only to trot."

"I thought he'd be easier to handle if I let him canter a bit. I didn't know he'd gallop like that."

Halsey shook his head. "You gotta learn to do what your trainer says. You wouldn't last two minutes at a racing stable. Anyways, he sure won't go to my ten-year-old grandson."

Middie's throat contracted. "What are you going to do with him?"

He grinned. "Mizz Bailey says as long as you don't mind extra work, he can stay here till I sell him. It won't be easy finding him a buyer. You keep ridin' him, long as you do what Mizz Bailey says."

Middie whooped for joy. "Oh, Halsey, I will, I will. I'll take supergood care of him."

"You'd better." He took off his hat and ran his fingers through his gray hair. "Funny thing about that horse. I got him because they said he was a good horse for a kid. But he sure puts me in mind of a racehorse at the farm where I used to work, twenty some years ago. This big fella is marked exactly like that horse, that funny star like a kite."

Middie's heart skipped a beat. "Maybe it's the same horse."

Halsey shook his head. "It can't be. That horse was put down after an accident. Too bad, because he'd got to be a famous Event horse back East."

"Oh," said Middie.

"Well, I'll keep lookin' for a good horse for my grandson. You ride this one all you can."

"Oh, I will, every day!" Now she would be able to enter him in a show. Holiday was a marvelous jumper — with him, she would have a good chance to win some ribbons and make Laurie proud of her. And then a thought struck her so suddenly, she caught her breath. If he was still at their barn in October, she could enter him at Idlewood!

She was aware of a silence. Janet rolled her eyes.

Halsey was grinning at her. "I was sayin' we'll prob'ly never find out his real name. All I know is, he was a racehorse. His lip is tattooed but it's so old now, I can't read it."

"Oh," said Middie. In her head, the word *Idlewood* danced around and around.

Halsey took a bandanna out of his pocket and wiped his face. "Mizz Bailey, I thank you for keepin' him for me."

Middie looked up at the old lady leaning on the porch railing. "This is the best summer I'll ever have in my whole life. I'll do everything I can to thank you for it."

Mrs. Bailey frowned. "You can start by following orders next time." She looked at Middie's face shining with happiness, and her frown softened. "We'll put that horse on a good training schedule. He needs lots of love and a great deal of work. We'll see how far you can go with him."

Middie nodded. "Okay by me. And I'll follow orders."

Janet said, "You'd better be awfully careful."

Middie laughed. "I will." She put her chin up. "And I'll get him to jump that ravine before I'm through."

10.
Not Holiday. No.

In the three weeks after Holiday's refusal at the gully in the canyon, Middie tried hard to forget that part of the ride. He had been so great flying up the canyon and clearing every other obstacle. She thought again of the thrill she'd felt when she realized he was racing and jumping across country, not running away.

"What do you suppose Mrs. Jamison thinks about Peaches now?" asked Janet. She was sitting in the grass in Mrs. Jamison's backyard, her back against a huge cottonwood tree, watching Middie ride the beautiful palomino mare.

Middie was wondering how soon she could enter Holiday in a show. She was sure he would be at Mrs. Bailey's at least another month.

"Well?" asked Janet.

"What did you say?"

"I was wondering what Mrs. Jamison thinks about Peaches now. She doesn't bomb out anymore like she used to."

Middie began walking the mare to cool her out.

"She is better, isn't she? I don't know what Mrs. Jamison thinks, but I'll find out soon. She brings me my check at Mrs. Bailey's, and we talk about Peaches and decide what to do next."

"I want to hear what she says."

"What for?"

"I want to hear her say how good you've made Peaches."

Middie giggled. "Well, Peaches had to get better; she couldn't have gotten worse." It was nice knowing even Janet could see the change. She'd miss Janet at the end of the summer. They had a lot of fun together, even at the beach.

Janet wiggled up and down to scratch her back on the ridges of the tree trunk. "I don't know how you do it — get on horses that are so hard to ride, and have a good time doing it."

"It's kind of fun once I'm in the saddle." She gave Peaches some slaps of affection. The palomino dropped her head and nickered softly. "There's a really good horse show at Val Verde a few weeks from now, in mid-August. A lot of riders use it as a prep for Idlewood. I was hoping I might enter Peaches, but that was before I got Holiday. I sure wish I could enter him."

"Why do you think about horse showing all the time? Horse showing is such a pain. I hate it."

Middie was so surprised, she was sure she'd heard wrong. She dropped her stirrups and swung off the horse. "What did you say?"

"I said I *hate* horse showing."

Middie stood silent a moment. "But you ride in shows a lot! Why in the world do you keep showing if you don't like it?"

Janet twisted a lock of her hair around one finger. "It's my mother. Mom is crazy over horse shows. She wanted a horse when she was little, and she thinks I'm just like her. I used to love horses, but it's no fun riding anymore." She dropped her hands in her lap. "I guess I'm scared something will happen."

"For somebody who's scared, you ride awfully well to win so many shows."

"Yeah, well, Mom got me a good trainer. Mom says he's the best for miles around."

"How did you ever get into horse showing?"

Janet's voice was so low, Middie could barely hear her. "Daddy gave me a pony. She was the gentlest, dearest pony you ever saw, and I really loved her. But then Mom made me enter her in a horse show, and the judge wouldn't look at my pony in the ring. Mom was so mad! She sold my pony and bought me a horse."

"Wow! Just like that you got a horse. Lucky you!"

"Well, I don't know. Mom and Dad had a fight about that. And then the horse gave me a bad fright, and I wanted to quit riding. Mom kept getting different horses for me until she found one I could ride without being too scared. Since I have to ride, I guess I'm lucky having Minaret."

"Gee!" exclaimed Middie. "I wish my mom liked horse showing like your mom."

"We ought to trade," said Janet, and they laughed. "I still miss that pony, but my trainer says you can't be sentimental if you want to win. I wish I didn't *have* to win."

"Why don't you tell your mother?"

Janet sighed. "I did, but she never listens to me. She tells me what kind of clothes I like to wear, what colors I like best, what things I like doing. When I win, it's sort of like her winning instead. It's really what *she* wants, and not me at all." A smile flickered across her face. "Sometimes I think you know me better than my own mother does."

"I guess I don't want to trade mothers." At least Middie's mother let her choose a lot of things herself. When Middie had told her she was going to give Laurie a landscape oil painting for her birthday, her mother looked surprised and happy and said, "How lovely, Middie. I'm sure she'll be pleased."

Middie was counting a lot on that landscape painting. She wanted Laurie to be impressed. Which reminded her . . . "I'd better go home and finish my painting. I want to give it to Laurie on Saturday."

"You said her birthday was Sunday."

"It is. But she might want to show it to her friends at the party." Anyway, Middie hoped so.

"Don't forget you're having an overnight with me that night."

"I won't forget. Laurie said she didn't want anything that smelled like a horse at her party. I told her that horses smell good."

"But you're not a horse," Janet pointed out. They laughed.

Laurie's eighteenth birthday party was going to be very special — dinner with dancing afterward. Weeks ago there had been wailing from Laurie over the guest list — she had so many friends — but her mother said they had to draw the line somewhere. There was going to be live music, a three-piece band that all Laurie's friends liked. Her mom was making Laurie a new white dress for the party, and they were going to rent card tables and colored tablecloths and everything. The house had been in an uproar all week while Laurie and her mom were getting it ready, but Middie didn't mind. She stayed at the barns all day long with Janet and rode as much as she could.

The painting would be nice, but if only, Middie said to herself, if only I could do something spectacular. Idlewood was so far in the future, but the Val Verde Horse Show! It would be wonderful if she could enter Holiday in it. Some day when Holiday had been especially good, Middie would ask Mrs. Bailey.

On Wednesday, she thought she had her chance.

"Very nice, Middie," Mrs. Bailey said when Middie had sponged and scraped the thorough-bred and turned him loose. "Holiday is making real progress."

"I was wondering if I could enter him at Val Verde next month. Would that be okay?"

Mrs. Bailey shook her head firmly. "Absolutely not."

Middie gulped. "Why not?"

"Holiday isn't ready to enter anything yet."

Middie tried to keep her voice from rising. "He's doing awfully well, and this is probably my only chance to show him. I won't have him forever."

"You won't be able to show that horse for an-other four or five months, at least. You have a lot of riding to do before he's calm enough for a show."

"But he's sort of calm. Please, Mrs. Bailey. It's a benefit for the Children's Hospital, and my family might even go and watch me ride. They've never seen me in a show." She said slowly, "I've never had a horse good enough."

"Oh." Mrs. Bailey studied her face. "It's a worthy cause, I won't argue that. But if you want to enter Val Verde, you might consider Peaches. You'd be far better off with her. Not Holiday. No."

Middie sank down onto the bench by the barn. "I wanted to enter Holiday. Peaches isn't nearly as good as Holiday."

"Peaches has improved quite a bit. You'd better think about her. I'll talk to Mrs. Jamison."

Middie looked up. "You mean that?"

Mrs. Bailey nodded. "I think she might say yes. You've been very good for Peaches."

Middie wondered if Mrs. Jamison really would let her ride the palomino in a show. Mrs. Jamison was funny. She was so fussy about Peaches and loved her a lot, even though riding the mare made her nervous. Suppose she said yes. . . . The mare was a natural jumper, not as good as Holiday, but Middie might have a chance at some ribbons.

"I'll phone her tonight and see." Mrs. Bailey smiled. "That will give you plenty of time to send in your entry."

Middie jumped to her feet. "Oh, boy! Oh, boy! If only she'll say yes!"

11.
Val Verde,
Here I Come

"It's true — Peaches is much easier for me to ride now," Mrs. Jamison had said to Mrs. Bailey on the phone. "I can see why Middie would want to take her to Val Verde. I'll talk to Joshua Logan after my next lesson, and I'll let you know."

Friday morning was lesson time for Middie and Peaches. Mrs. Bailey always drove her ancient, cream-colored Packard to the Jamisons' for the lesson. She drove very slowly, holding the wheel gently but firmly as though she were holding reins, looking with calm eyes over the top of it. The girls sat in the back on the velvet upholstery and pretended they were rich and Mrs. Bailey was a chauffeur in uniform. People always turned around to stare at the car. Middie didn't know how old it was; she knew it looked different from any other car she'd ever seen. The paint was so bright and the chrome so glittery that sometimes even Peaches spooked at it.

Mrs. Bailey parked the car carefully on the driveway where she had a clear view of the whole backyard. She gave the girls instructions for setting up an eight-obstacle course.

The course was very difficult. Middie concentrated hard, and managed to get Peaches around with a clean go and several smooth fences. After the lesson, Mrs. Bailey smiled at Middie. "Next time, use the corners of your ring a little more. Other than that, it was all right."

"I *told* you Peaches was getting good," said Janet as they drove back to Mrs. Bailey's. "I'll bet Mrs. Jamison isn't half as scared of her as she used to be."

Middie grinned. "We'll find out tomorrow! Let's pack lunches so we can hang around at Mrs. Bailey's till Mrs. Jamison calls back."

In the morning, Middie rode Holiday, working on transitions between gaits. She was pleased when Mrs. Bailey said she could see quite an improvement. After Middie put Holiday away, she and Janet retired to the cool shade of the barn with their brown paper bags and cans of soda pop.

They liked to eat in the barn, sitting on bales of sweet-smelling alfalfa with another bale for a table.

Middie licked peanut butter and jelly from her fingers and started on a cupcake with white frosting and chocolate sprinkles. "I hope she doesn't forget to call."

"She'll call."

"I hope she says yes."

Janet rolled her eyes. "She'll say yes."

But the afternoon dragged on. Middie cleaned Holiday's bridle and was almost through cleaning his saddle before the telephone rang. Very shortly Mrs. Bailey stepped onto the front porch and called out, "She says yes! You can enter Peaches at Val Verde!"

"Yippee! Yippee!" shouted Middie, dancing around the barnyard.

"I'm glad for you," said Janet. "I hope everything comes out all right."

"Sure it will. Now I'll finish cleaning the saddle."

"I thought you wanted to hurry home," Janet said. "Today is Laurie's party, remember? Aren't you going to give her that oil painting today?"

Middie groaned. "I was going to, but I didn't quite finish it last night. There was a good program on TV about wild mustangs."

"I saw that, too. I loved seeing the little colts."

"Yeah, well, all I need is another hour or so. Can I finish it at your house?"

Janet nodded. "Aunt Elizabeth won't mind, especially since you're having an overnight with me."

The two girls hopped on their bicycles and started down the driveway. Middie glanced back at the barn. She didn't remember fastening the chain on Derry's paddock. "Wait up for me," she called to Janet. She ran to the barnyard and looked. The chain was fastened securely. "I might have known," she said out loud, and ran back to her bike.

Middie didn't know their house could look so beautiful. Dinner was going to be a buffet, with the food laid out on the dining table. On the patio, the card tables were set up for eating. Middie paused in the doorway. It looked like somebody else's house, with baskets of fresh flowers on each card table, and tall candles glowing in colored glass columns to match the different-colored linen tablecloths. Middie wondered if she would ever enjoy that kind of party.

Her mother came into the living room. "Did you wipe your shoes real well? Don't touch a thing until you wash."

"Okay," said Middie. "Keep Laurie in the kitchen for a couple of minutes, will you? I'm going to sneak my painting over to Janet's to finish."

"It's not finished?" said her mother, surprised.

"I haven't had time."

"You've had months and months to do it." Her mother sighed. "Either you race through things, or put them off. I don't understand you at all."

Middie shrugged and raced down the hallway. She had posted a big "Keep Out" sign on the door to her room. She closed the door behind her and looked at the painting on the easel. It was good — really good. Laurie *had* to like it. All Middie needed to do was touch up the eucalyptus trees and put in more sunlit grass in the foreground.

Middie threw a couple of brushes and paint tubes and rags into her paint box. She carried the box in one hand and with the other, gingerly picked up the wet canvas by its wooden frame. She hurried down the hall, through the patio between the colorful tablecloths and chairs, and shot out the side door to Janet's.

Mrs. Willoughby examined her handiwork. "I had no idea you painted so well, Middie. You're going to be a real artist."

Middie shrugged modestly. "I wish my family thought so. Thanks for letting me finish it here." She looked at it critically. "Darn. Look at that smudge. I must have smeared it on my way over. I'll have to fix that."

"Laurie should be proud to show that to her friends," Mrs. Willoughby said. "Are you giving it to her tonight?"

Middie shook her head. "It's not done yet. I'll have to give it to her in the morning."

They had a quiet supper together, with the sounds of the party drifting across the lawn from her own house. After supper she worked on her painting while she thought about Peaches and the Val Verde Show. She'd clean her room so if she won a ribbon, it would look nice on the wall. Wouldn't her mother be surprised!

Sunday morning she awoke in the twin bed beside Janet's, surprised that she had slept so well. She had thought the sound of the dance band next door would have kept her awake, but she hadn't even heard the band.

She looked out the window. The morning was bright, sunny, and clear. It was a perfect day for giving Laurie the painting. She could hardly wait. She wanted to hear Laurie say, "Why, Middie, how beautiful! I didn't know you could paint like that!"

12.
The Awful
Birthday Party

Middie was too excited to eat breakfast. She hurried to her house with the finished painting. The house was silent. Of course, they were sleeping in. She set the canvas on the kitchen table and began writing a note to Laurie.

There was a sound behind her, like a gasp. She turned. Laurie stood in the doorway in her robe and slippers, and her face was swollen from crying.

"Meredith Scott, I hate you! You are the most awful sister anybody ever had!"

Middie stared. "What did I do?"

"You ruined my party. Absolutely ruined it."

"I wasn't even there!"

Laurie pointed an accusing finger at the painting. "That started it. The paint was wet when you carried it through the patio, and you got paint on one of the tablecloths. Oil paint!"

"So that's how it happened," said Middie. "I wondered how it got smeared."

"That's not all!" said Laurie, her voice rising.

"There was the green paint on the tablecloth, and I didn't see it, and it got all over the front of my new white dress." She pulled a tissue from her pocket and wiped her nose. "My beautiful white dress that Mom made just for the party. I had to wear an *old* dress instead!"

Middie cleared her throat. "Can't paint thinner get it out?"

"You *LOSER*!" yelled Laurie. "And *that's* not *all*! Guess what happened when we cleared the tables and rolled up the rugs to dance! Just guess!"

"Uh-oh," said Middie, recollection growing. "I guess I spilled a little paint a while back. I was going to . . ."

"A *little* paint!" Laurie's voice broke. "It was at least a gallon! And it must have been there a month! Covered up with newspapers — and they were stuck all over the floor like cement! The floor where we were going to dance!"

Middie couldn't think of anything to say.

Laurie said, "It's the only room in the house big enough to dance in, so there wasn't really any place to dance. The party broke up early, but Daddy had to pay the band anyway. I wanted to make you come home and start cleaning up but I was so mad, Mom wouldn't let me. She'll say plenty to you later. I've never had a worse time in my whole life."

Middie cleared her throat.

Laurie went on, "I'm tired of your always being in a hurry to get what *you* want. You never think about anybody else. All you care about is showing off in front of the Riding Club kids to put them down. You never take the time to do anything right, and everybody else has to pay for it. Someday I hope *you*'ll be the one to pay."

Middie found her voice. She croaked, "I'm sorry. Really." She held out the painting as a kind of peace offering.

Laurie yelled, "I never ever want to see that awful picture as long as I live."

"Okay, okay," said Middie. She took the painting and walked back to Janet's in a daze.

"What happened?" Janet asked. "Didn't she like it?"

"I'll tell you later," said Middie thickly. "Let's go to Mrs. Bailey's."

Janet looked at Middie's face. "You bet."

At the barn, Middie went through the motions of grooming Holiday, but she felt numb. She shivered a little as she saddled him.

When Middie rode yesterday she had thought that Holiday was nervous, but he was worse today. She had to struggle with him at every step. He stiffened his jaw, stuck his head up, and bent his neck the wrong way.

Janet sat silent with her arms wrapped around her knees, a puzzled look on her face.

Mrs. Bailey watched for a few minutes, pushed her cane against the ground, and stood up. "Middie," she called, "I want you to dismount right away and cool that horse out and put him away!"

Middie brought the horse to a walk and went back to Mrs. Bailey. "How come?"

"You know how come." Her voice was stern. "You are very upset, and you are upsetting the horse. You know better than to ride when you feel like that."

"All right." She swung off the horse and ran up her stirrups, then leaned against him for a minute. "I'm sorry, Holiday. I really am."

Mrs. Bailey cleared her throat. "Do you want to tell me about it?"

Middie shook her head and led the horse to the tie rail.

"Tomorrow is another day. You'll feel differently," the old lady said gently.

"I don't think so." She wanted to dig a hole and crawl into it. Just as she had thought she would impress Laurie and her family with her painting, she had ruined everything. *Everything*. Laurie would never forget it.

She sighed deeply and went through the motions of putting the horse and the tack away. When she came back from the tack room, Mrs. Bailey was still watching her.

"Thirty years from now you won't remember what happened," said the old lady. "No use crying over spilt milk."

Middie choked. "How about crying over spilled paint?"

"Spilled paint?"

Middie nodded. "Well, I . . ." She swallowed

hard. She had been awful. Really awful. How could she tell Mrs. Bailey what she had done? But how could she not?

She cleared her throat. "It started the day I came over here and first saw Holiday. I was supposed to clean up the patio first . . ." she began, "but I didn't."

Janet raised her head and stared, fascinated. Mrs. Bailey pressed her lips together in a straight line and listened in silence while Middie told her story.

Middie sighed again and finished. "So when Laurie said she didn't ever want to see my painting, I took it back to Janet's and left it there."

"And then?" asked Mrs. Bailey.

"And then I came over here."

Silence.

"You didn't go back home? You just walked *out*?"

Middie's voice wavered. "I guess I did. I'm sorry."

"Sorry, are you?" snapped Mrs. Bailey. "It doesn't look to me like you're sorry. Words won't do." Her voice was firm. "I thought you knew that the best way to take a fence is to face it and drive." Her cane stomped disapproval as she went back to the house.

Janet gave Middie a quick look of pity and followed.

Middie sat down on a bale of hay, trying to readjust her mind. She hadn't thought of it like an obstacle, a fence to jump, but it was. The worst part of it was that she hadn't even had a refusal; she'd had a run-out. And a run-out is always the rider's fault. Lack of control. A little frown crossed her face, and she sat still for a long time. At last she stood up and squared her shoulders.

She marched up to the house and into the living room. "Let's go home, Jan," she said. She met Mrs. Bailey's cool gray eyes. "I have a lot to do. I'd better get started."

The two girls rode their bikes back home in silence. Middie's mother was silent while she stammered her apologies. Middie remembered Mrs. Bailey's "words won't do." "Can I take the dress to the cleaners?" she asked.

"Laurie took it down this morning."

"Oh." She rubbed one ankle with the other foot. "I'll pay for it. And the band, too."

"You don't need to pay for the band, Middie," her mother said.

"Yes, I do. I want to." She lifted her chin a little. "What's good for getting that paint off the floor?"

"The floor cleaner and the scrub brush are under the kitchen sink; the bucket's in the garage. I'm afraid the paint has stained the wood; it may have to be sanded."

"I'll pay for that, too. It can come out of my horse fund."

Her mother looked startled. "It will be very expensive. Do you really mean that?"

"That's okay. I don't have time for a horse of my own right now. I'm going to work hard on Peaches. Mrs. Jamison is letting me enter her in the Val Verde Horse Show in mid-August."

"My goodness," her mother said. "That's the big benefit for the Children's Hospital, isn't it?"

Middie nodded. She didn't have the nerve to ask her mother and father to go. Not after what she had just done.

Her mother had an odd look on her face. "Well, paying all the bills won't make Laurie's party right, but at least you're taking some responsibility for your actions." She paused. "Maybe we ought to come and watch you ride."

13.
Horse Show Rules

"**M**iddie, you'd better keep your mind on that horse," declared Janet, hastily sliding off the fence as Holiday whirled around a few inches from where Janet had been sitting.

It was good advice. Middie's excitement was transferred to the horse. Holiday pranced, jigged sideways, and looked for any excuse to break away.

"I'll have to lead him to cool him out," said Middie, sliding from the saddle. "I guess I was thinking about the Val Verde Show, and that's why he won't settle down." She wondered if Holiday would ever be as well-behaved as Peaches.

"Probably not," she said to him and scratched his neck just back of his jaw. He nickered softly and stretched out his neck for more. Middie led him to the tie rail.

Janet sighed and shook her head. "You and my mother are just alike. All you ever think about is horse showing."

Middie took off Holiday's bridle and slipped the halter over his head. "Yeah, but for different reasons." She unbuckled the girth.

Janet frowned. "I suppose so. Mom's trying to make me win because *she* wants to win." She twisted a lock of hair around one finger. "You want to win to make your family proud of you."

Middie disappeared into the tack room with the saddle. She slid it onto the rack and stood there a moment, silent. It was more than making her family proud. She'd never told anyone how it felt being the Caboose.

Middie came back into the sunlight and picked up the bucket and sponge.

"I sure hope you win at Val Verde," said Janet.

Middie squeezed the sponge over the horse's back. "I never told you. It just so happens that my sisters and my brother didn't really want me when I was born. I came along by accident six years after Laurie."

Janet's eyebrows went up. "Good grief! How awful!" She stared at Middie. "But they want you now, don't they?"

Middie kept on sponging and scraping.

"Don't they?"

"How should I know? It seems to me I'm always messing things up for Laurie or Karen. Like the birthday party. If only I could do something spectacular to make them feel differently."

"Oh," said Janet. "Now I get it. They'll be glad you're in the family if you're a great rider."

"Yeah. Now you see why winning is so important."

Janet nodded her head vigorously. "I sure do. It must be awful to feel like you're not really wanted. I'll help you all I can. Maybe I can be your groom at Val Verde."

"That's neat. Sure!" Middie smiled. She couldn't imagine Janet grooming even Peaches. But it made her feel good having Janet on her side.

The girls turned around at the sound of a car coming up the driveway. It was a two-tone brown Blazer.

"That's Mrs. Jamison's car," exclaimed Middie. "I guess today is payday." She couldn't explain why she suddenly felt uneasy.

They saw a short slender figure hop out of the Blazer. Mrs. Jamison, wearing boots and breeches and a green polo shirt, went bouncing into Mrs. Bailey's house. Middie finished putting Holiday away, and she and Janet hurried up the steps.

Mrs. Bailey met them at the front door. "Mrs. Jamison has some good news for you, Middie," she said, but Middie could tell from her face that it wasn't really good news.

Mrs. Jamison's face was small like a pixie's, and her blue eyes were round and shining with excitement. "I've just had another lesson on Peaches from Joshua Logan, and he says we both have improved so much that I can ride her in the Val Verde Show! You can still go in the Junior classes with her."

"That's wonderful!" exclaimed Middie. She drew in her breath and wondered what was coming next.

"This morning we jumped three feet six beautifully. I'm entering the Amateur-Owner classes!"

"Oh!" Middie and Janet looked at each other quickly. Middie felt as though someone had punched her in the stomach. She sat down carefully in the nearest chair. Now she knew what was wrong. Horse Show rules. Mrs. Jamison didn't know that a horse entered in Amateur-Owner classes isn't allowed to be entered in the Junior Division, too.

Mrs. Bailey smiled at Mrs. Jamison. "I'm very happy for you, Carol. Middie should be proud of what she has done for your mare."

Janet kept looking at Middie, motioning her to say something about the rule. Middie pretended not to see her.

Mrs. Jamison was still bubbling over. "You should have seen Peaches this morning. I didn't have a bit of trouble on the whole course, even on the turns after the fences."

"That's great," said Middie with an effort. "I remember when you were scared to jump more than two little bitty fences in a row."

Mrs. Jamison laughed. "You've worked wonders with my dear horse. I'll trailer her to Val Verde, and you can come along in my Blazer if you want."

Janet opened her mouth to speak. Middie shot

her a warning look and smiled at Mrs. Jamison. "Thanks a lot. I'll have to think about that."

"By the way, here's your check. And here's a little extra for giving me the chance to ride Peaches in a show at last. I'm sure you can find something to spend it on, getting ready for Val Verde."

Middie kept the smile pasted onto her face. She looked down at the envelope and pulled out a check and a fifty-dollar bill. "Mrs. Jamison, you shouldn't have done that."

"I wanted to. I'm so happy, and it's mostly because of you." She started for the door and waved to them.

"Well, thanks a lot, Mrs. Jamison. I'll see you."

The Blazer backed down the driveway while Mrs. Bailey and the girls sat in their chairs. After a few moments of silence, Mrs. Bailey cleared her throat. "You didn't tell her."

"Tell her what?" Middie tried to look innocent.

"The Horse Show Association rules. You know perfectly well you can't ride Peaches in the Junior Division if she's entered in the Amateur-Owner classes."

"Yeah, I know." Middie's face crumpled. "Why did this have to happen to me?" Her eyes blurred. "I don't want her ole money. I wanted to ride Peaches in the show."

Mrs. Bailey's voice was calm. "You can explain to her about the rule, you know. There are other classes she can enter that wouldn't keep you from riding Peaches."

"But she wants to go in Amateur-Owner. She's so happy about it. She'll have a better chance there than in the Open classes." She fished in her jeans and pulled out a tissue. "I can't ask her not to, especially when she's always been so nice to me." She blew her nose. "I won't send in my entry."

"That's not fair! That's not fair at all," Janet burst out. "You've *got* to go to Val Verde."

"What's that?" asked Mrs. Bailey.

"Nothing," Middie said quickly. "She thinks I'm as nutty about showing as her mother is. I mean as she is."

"And you're not?" said Mrs. Bailey.

Middie stared out the window. "I don't want Mrs. Jamison to know what's happened. She'd change her entry so I could ride. She's that kind of a lady. And I'm not going to spoil Val Verde for her."

Mrs. Bailey nodded. "I see. You're certain you want it this way?"

Middie was silent for a minute. "I'm sure."

"What reason will you give her?"

It really wasn't fair, that all her hard work with Peaches would be the very thing to keep her from entering the show her family was going to see. But there wasn't any way out. She put her head in her hands. "I'll think of something. Just as long as Mrs. Jamison doesn't find out the real reason."

14.
Val Verde
After All

Mrs. Bailey looked hard at Middie. "I know you've counted on Val Verde for a long time."

Middie shrugged. "So what? I'll survive. I just have to think of a good reason to tell Mrs. Jamison."

Mrs. Bailey pushed her cane against the floor and stood up. "Perhaps I can give you a good reason. How would you like to enter Holiday?"

Middie gasped. *"What?* But you told me I couldn't — that he wouldn't be ready for months!"

"That's true, but sometimes we have to do things even when we're not ready. It certainly won't be easy for you, but if you're willing to ride Holiday at Val Verde, I'll see that Halsey will let you enter him."

Middie leapt from her chair. "Wow! That's fantastic!"

"That's terrible!" exclaimed Janet. "That horse

is downright dangerous for Middie to ride in a show!"

Mrs. Bailey smiled. "Let's give Middie a chance, shall we? It's important to her to keep Mrs. Jamison happy. I can't think of a better reason for letting her take Holiday to Val Verde."

Janet's face showed worry lines as she shook her head. "I wanted her to go to Val Verde, but not on Holiday. Middie, you've never ridden him in a crowd at all. You don't know what he'll do!"

"Don't worry, Jan," said Middie, dancing around the room. "We'll do just fine together."

Two weeks later, in the cab of Halsey's pickup truck, Middie wasn't so sure. The horse trailer jiggled and squeaked behind them, and through the green glass window Middie saw Holiday's head from time to time as he looked up from his alfalfa.

At least *he*'s not nervous, thought Middie. She'd been so confident before, but now that they were actually here, she was filled with doubts.

As the truck went around a corner, Middie swallowed hard and waved to her family and Mrs. Bailey in the station wagon following the horse trailer. Middie's plan had worked — not only had her parents come, but Laurie, too.

Mrs. Bailey smiled and gestured in return.

I'll bet she knows I'm scared, thought Middie, but she won't let on. If I blow it, she won't blame me. Middie sighed. Laurie would say I shouldn't have entered.

The truck turned off the highway and rattled between big stone pillars into the show grounds. Middie straightened up. This was the best chance she'd ever had to impress her family.

Miles of horse trailers were already parked in the meadow when they arrived. In the early sunlight the fences sparkled white, and the oak trees cast deep shadows along the paths where blanketed horses were being led up and down. A row of colored flags billowed across the top of the little grandstand.

Middie backed Holiday down the ramp and tied him to the side of the trailer.

Holiday stared at the flags and the crowds and all the horses and shivered with excitement. He remembered the many times when Brian had ridden him through crowds like this into an arena. Sometimes there were towering fences to jump, and his heart pounded with anticipation.

Holiday swung around at the trailer and began blowing and whinnying. Middie tried to calm him by brushing him.

She had spent a long time bathing and clipping and grooming the horse. She had had to pull his mane before braiding it, and she hated pulling manes. It took forever.

As usual, she had tried to hurry through the job, not bothering with the comb. Too late she discovered her little fingers on both hands were blistered and bleeding from the coarse hair. She sighed. Why couldn't she learn to take her time? Mrs. Bailey said nothing, but patched her up with Band-Aids. Her fingers still hurt.

She had taken her time braiding him, though, and he was beautiful. He had put on weight from the A and M, and his coat shone like iridescent copper in the morning sun. As she tacked him up, her heart pounded with pride. Even Janet said he looked super.

Janet fussed over Middie, fixing her hair, making sure her hunt cap was on just so, straightening her stock tie.

"This is a horse show, not a beauty contest," said Middie, giggling nervously.

"But you have to make a good impression on the judge," declared Janet. "I'll wipe your boots off just before you go in the ring."

Middie smiled. "I'm sure glad you're here with me."

"Me, too," said Janet happily.

Middie leaned over and said in a low voice, "There's one more reason I wanted to enter Holiday in this show."

"What's that?" Janet whispered back.

"A lot of the Riding Club kids are here. Holiday is the first really good horse that they've seen me ride."

Janet was puzzled. "So?"

Middie hesitated. "When I was taking lessons

at the Club, I always got the crummiest of the school horses, the ones nobody else wanted to ride because they had rough gaits, or they didn't like to jump. My instructor knew my family didn't have a lot of money to spend. And, besides, the kids always stared at my boots because they weren't leather."

Janet was silent. "I didn't know that." She looked at Middie and said fiercely, "I hope you win. I want you to beat *everybody*!" They smiled at each other, and Janet held up two fingers for victory.

Middie led Holiday over to Mrs. Bailey, who was sitting under an oak tree studying the program.

"You have lots of time before your first class — hunt seat equitation. Go settle him down a bit and be ready for your call."

"For us it's only a warm-up before the jumping class," said Middie anxiously. "I hope my family . . ."

Mrs. Bailey nodded. "I told them Holiday is not an equitation horse, and not to expect a thing."

"Thank goodness," said Middie, relieved. She swung up into the saddle. "Wish me luck."

Janet carefully wiped the dust from Middie's boots with a towel. She looked up at Middie and said earnestly, "I do, oh, I do!"

"Good luck," said Mrs. Bailey. She smiled, and her gray eyes suddenly sparkled. "Have a good ride!"

Holiday danced sideways as Middie rode him into the main ring with the other horses. She pushed him forward into a trot, and reluctantly he let her swing him into line. Soon all the riders were trotting steadily in a big circle in the arena.

There weren't any jumps in the ring. Holiday remembered going into the arena a number of times with other horses when there weren't any jumps. Those classes didn't hold any excitement for him. He flattened his ears, switched his tail, and began tossing his head.

Middie wished she knew what was wrong. Several times he almost broke to a canter, and Middie wondered for a minute if he just wanted to get the class over with. She kept checking him to the trot, and tried not to let him lean so hard on the bit. Holiday snorted, flared his nostrils, and suddenly lengthened his trot stride.

Middie groaned to herself. If she tried to slow him down, she knew he would argue and end up by tossing his head even more. She steered him carefully away from the other horses as they flew by.

Middie caught sight of a blonde girl riding a shining big brown horse. If it was who she thought it was, Middie was in for trouble. As they went skimming by, Middie took a second glance — yes, it was Tyler Benning, the girl who had always made Middie's life miserable at the Riding Club. Middie almost wished she'd never heard of Val Verde.

The most important thing now was to keep away from Tyler.

15.
Tyler, Mike, and Susie

Holiday didn't want to walk or trot or canter in the ring; he wanted to gallop. From time to time he bounded and spun to break free, but Middie didn't give up trying to make him behave. Each minute she expected to be excused and sent out of the ring, but she wasn't. When the riders lined up, and the judge announced the awards, Holiday almost stood still. At last it was over. Middie took a deep breath and started to leave the arena.

Tyler Benning had stopped at the gate to hand her ribbon to someone, and her horse was partly blocking the way. The other riders bunched up, trying to go around. Before Middie could stop him, Holiday danced into the group and crowded against the brown horse.

Tyler's head swiveled around. "Mind your manners!" she snapped.

"I'm sorry." Middie wanted to sink into the ground.

Someone said, "Move it, Tyler. You're blocking the gate."

Tyler moved her horse to one side, looked again at Middie, and smiled. "I remember you. You took lessons at the Club and always rode those weird horses that wouldn't jump."

Middie tried to stay cool. "They jumped just fine after I rode them awhile."

"Really?" Tyler shifted her reins. "I only remember how funny you looked."

Middie clenched her teeth. She wheeled Holiday away and headed for Mrs. Bailey.

The old lady was smiling broadly. "Well, you stayed for the entire class, and you left the ring together. On Holiday, that's quite an accomplishment." Her smile faded. "What happened?"

"Nothing." Middie's eyes were stinging. She blurted out, "I can't *stand* that girl on the brown horse. She's so *awful* to me."

Mrs. Bailey nodded. "I saw her — she's the kind who sheds blood for blue ribbons. There's someone like that in every horse show. Keep your mind on your own horse, and do your best. If she's trying to upset you, it means she thinks you're real competition."

"Oh," said Middie. She felt much better. Mrs. Bailey didn't miss a thing. Middie smiled and pointed beyond the staging area. "They've posted the course for the Junior Jumpers. I'll go look at it and tell you what it's like."

A group of riders was gathered around the charts tacked up on the barn. Middie rode Holiday into the group and peered over their shoulders. A plump girl on a shining fat little Morgan moved over to give Middie room. The girl wore pigtails and a bright blue coat and she looked worried.

"Well, the Junior Jumpers course looks pretty good," said Tyler Benning's voice.

The plump girl beside Middie spoke up. "That's an awful combination at the end. It sure looks hard."

"What do you care?" said Tyler. "You'll never get that far," and everyone laughed, even the plump girl.

The girl's round face smiled up at Middie. "It's true, you know. I'm terrible in the ring. My pony knows I'm scared. We do okay out in the field because he loves to gallop, but in the ring I hardly ever get over more than three or four fences. I keep hoping the next time will be better, but it never is." She turned her pony to leave and said in a cheerful voice, "Here goes nothing."

"I don't know why she doesn't give up," said Tyler, smirking. "She's too chicken to make her pony jump. What a dunce."

"Blood for blue ribbons," Mrs. Bailey had said about Tyler.

Middie squared her shoulders. "If she's scared and keeps on trying, she's really brave."

Tyler gave Middie a withering look. "She's not brave, just stupid." She looked down at Middie's hands and burst out laughing. "Look at her hands, everybody," she called out. She pointed to the Band-Aids. "Blisters from pulling his mane, I bet." She smiled sweetly at Middie. "You're even greener than I thought. Do you think you'll make it over the first fence?"

Middie stared straight ahead, her face frozen. She hated the Riding Club kids, and she hated Tyler Benning most of all.

"And over here on my right, ladies and gentlemen," said a boy's voice behind her, "we have the great Tyler Benning. She was born knowing it all, so she never had to learn how to ride like the rest of us."

There was a silence followed by a small ripple of laughter from the other riders. Tyler bit her lip and turned her horse away. Middie looked around cautiously at the boy who had spoken.

He was sitting on a dark bay thoroughbred. He looked a couple of years older than Middie, and she could tell he was a lot taller. He was very thin, with reddish-brown hair curling above his coat collar, and his face completely covered with freckles. He winked solemnly at Middie. "That's a good-looking animal you have," he said. "How does he jump?"

"Like a bomb," said Middie, swallowing hard. She added quickly, "It's my first show with him, but he's been around. I'm counting on him to make up for me."

The boy laughed. "Sounds like a plan." He waggled his eyebrows. "If this is our lucky day, Tyler will fall off." They both laughed. He said, "Have a good ride."

When he rode away, Middie finished studying the course and went to look for the plump girl on the Morgan. In the warm-up ring Middie found her and rode alongside.

"I think you're brave to keep trying."

The plump girl giggled. "Not really. I am kind of dumb, I guess. But I meet some really neat boys at the shows."

Middie grinned. "You're not so dumb." They laughed. "Who's the redheaded boy on the big bay thoroughbred?"

"You don't know *him*?" asked the girl. "You *are* new. That's Mike Mitchell. His family raises racehorses. Mike's fourteen, I guess. His uncle helps him train his own hunters and jumpers from their horses off the track. He's got rooms full of trophies and ribbons. I think he's awesome."

Middie moaned. "I didn't want to get into competition like *that*. This is my first time in a show with this horse."

"Wait till you see *me* ride. You'll think it's my first time on a horse. My name's Susie Rooney. What's yours?"

"Meredith Scott. Middie." How could anyone stay scared with someone like Susie around? Middie's spirits rose. The girls halted to listen to the loudspeaker.

"Let's tie our horses to the trailer," said Susie. "They're calling for the course walk for Junior Jumpers. Come on!"

16.
Junior Jumpers

The fences looked enormous to Middie as she tramped around the course with the other competitors. A very thin man wearing a yellow polo shirt, tan breeches, and field boots led a group of riders around the course. Middie recognized Joshua Logan, Mrs. Jamison's instructor and a top trainer. He was explaining to his younger students the best way to ride the course. Middie walked behind his group, trying to hear what he was saying while she counted the number of strides between fences.

She was long-legged enough that her strides were much the same as Joshua's. That was *one* advantage to being tall. But the size of the fences scared her, especially the ones with spreads.

She reported her course walk to Mrs. Bailey, who had been watching her from the fence near the out-gate.

"Those fences are huge," moaned Middie, "and I'm not sure how he'll take those real fences after all the rinky-dink ones we've been practicing on at home."

"After your rinky-dink fences," said Mrs. Bailey, "your horse will enjoy jumping these. Let's go over the strides between fences and plan your strategy. You can count on Holiday getting excited. Your real problem won't be the fences —it will be controlling the horse."

As soon as Middie entered the ring the second time and made her circle, she forgot about being scared. Holiday pricked his ears and galloped through the starting flags.

How many times Brian had ridden him into an arena like this among towering fences! He recalled the excitement of attacking each obstacle, the thunderous applause from the crowds when he finished, and always the big pat afterward from Brian with the words, "Good job, Magic, good job!"

Now only silence throbbed in his head, but the excitement was all around him just the same, and the girl was legging him on just as Brian always did. She tried to bring him in at the right angle and impulsion, and when they were at the fence she tried not to interfere so he could figure out the best way to take it. Holiday began to snort happily with every stride.

Each time the horse sped up, Middie concentrated on collecting him or shortening his stride.

When he paid attention, he was fine. They had two knockdowns, which put her out of the ribbons.

"Those knockdowns were my fault," groaned Middie. "On the first one, I went too fast and let him get strung out."

"Pooh," exclaimed Susie. "Anybody can make that mistake."

Middie shook her head. "And on the second one, I brought him in too close for that big a jump."

"Good grief," Susie said. "You looked great. You looked like a real pro. Wish I could jump like that!"

Middie began to smile. "I want you to meet my trainer, Mrs. Bailey, and my family. And then maybe you can walk the Fault and Out course with me."

Susie beamed with pleasure. "Sure, let's go."

Back at the horse trailer the whole family was waiting, and Middie could feel their excitement growing.

"I didn't know you could ride like that," said Laurie, gingerly patting Holiday's neck.

Janet and Middie smiled at each other.

Middie's mother said, "You looked very nice, Middie. Your horse certainly flies over those fences."

Her father said, "You going out for the Indy 500 next?"

"Oh, Dad." Sometimes she wished he'd be serious.

Mrs. Bailey motioned Middie aside. "I suppose

you know why you had those knockdowns."

Middie nodded. "All my fault. I wasn't thinking just then."

To Middie's surprise, the old lady laughed. "The cure for that is more riding and more showing. The rest of your course was beautiful. I was very proud of you."

Middie's eyes opened wide. "Proud . . . of me?" she stammered.

"Certainly!" said Mrs. Bailey. "You are riding a very difficult horse and you made it look easy."

Middie felt like she was floating three feet above the ground. "Thanks," she whispered, not entirely trusting her voice.

"Oh, no!" exclaimed her mother. "They're raising all the jumps. Don't tell me you have to jump those."

Middie looked at the arena. "If it's the Fault and Out class, I do."

"What in the world is Fault and Out?"

Middie tried to look nonchalant. "That's where you get points for each jump you take clean," she explained. "You keep going until you have a knockdown. The winner is the horse with the most points and the fastest time." She saw there were several oxers, big wide fences with parallel bars at the top. She chewed uneasily on her lower lip.

"You ought to win that one hands down," said Janet. "I've never seen a horse jump as fast as Holiday."

Mrs. Bailey spoke up. "Yes, I believe Holiday

does have a good chance. The course is fairly straightforward. There might be a number of clean rounds, so the fastest time will determine the winner. After you've walked the course, let's figure out the best way to take it."

They found a place where there weren't many people, and Middie drew a diagram in the dirt. "The hardest part is going from the fifth to the sixth fence, the oxer and then the triple bar. They ought to be in a straight line, but they're not — they're on a bent line to make it harder."

"Very interesting," said Mrs. Bailey. "The more experienced riders will make an S curve between the two, and the rest will circle that other fence in order to come in straight to the triple." Mrs. Bailey studied the fences. "Holiday turns so quickly, you can certainly do the S curve, but it won't be easy."

"We can do the S if he's listening to me." Middie mentally measured the oxer and glanced at Mrs. Bailey.

The old lady was smiling. "There is one faster way to take those fences," she said, a faraway look in her eyes.

"What's that?" asked Middie.

"You could jump them as though they were in a straight line — take them one right after the other at an angle."

Middie's mouth made a big O. She gulped. "But that triple bar is so big, you'd never get a horse over it if you didn't come in straight."

"Unless you had a very gifted horse," said Mrs. Bailey calmly. "A horse like Holiday."

Middie felt goose bumps rise on her arms. "You think Holiday could take those two in line? He could get over that triple bar right from the oxer?"

"Yes, I think he could." Mrs. Bailey looked away as though she were watching a horse in some distant arena. "One of my Grand Prix horses, Jupiter, could have done that." Her gaze suddenly shifted to Middie's startled expression. "You'll need a lot of controlled power for the oxer and as you land, increase your speed for the triple. If it's two strides between the fences, Holiday can do it."

Middie shook her head.

"Why don't you go out and measure the distance between the two? Then we'll know just how difficult it is. Stride off to one side, so no one will guess what you have in mind."

Middie pretended to be measuring the S curve and the circle to the oxer, and came back to Mrs. Bailey. "I think it's a short three or two long strides, and that means Holiday would take two."

"Then he certainly could do it," said Mrs. Bailey.

"But I don't think *I* can."

Mrs. Bailey nodded. "Perhaps you're not ready for it. Perhaps you don't trust each other enough yet. But you can think about it."

Middie studied the little flags above the grandstands. They were fluttering gaily in the breeze that had come up.

"You're riding very well," Mrs. Bailey said, smiling.

Middie felt her face turn pink with pleasure.

"You'd better take one last look at the entire course." The old lady pointed to the charts posted on the barn. "Good luck, and remember you've got a good horse."

Middie didn't want to go back to look at the course charts. She already knew the course, and she had enough on her mind as it was. Her fingers shook ever so slightly as she untied Holiday from the trailer.

She could feel her heartbeats jarring the front of her hunt coat as she watched rider after rider take the course, each trying to go clean and still beat the clock. Some went too fast and knocked down a pole and were eliminated. Mike Mitchell, who had already won three blue ribbons, took his horse Jiffy over in a breathtaking performance, cutting every corner and racing between fences. He went clean, and the time was forty-two seconds. The crowd yelled approval. He had ridden the S curve between the oxer and the triple bar.

Forty-two seconds! Middie had watched him spin and turn with lightning speed. She couldn't possibly beat that.

Unless she took the oxer and the triple bar as though they were in line. Her scalp prickled at the thought of the risk; she had once seen a horse and rider fall at a triple bar and both got hurt. But Mrs. Bailey had said Holiday could do it. If Middie asked him to and he hesitated at all, they would certainly crash into the fence. Did he trust her enough not to hesitate?

17.
Over the Fence
and Out

Middie heard her number called, and she moved Holiday toward the gate. She shut her mind to the combination and concentrated on the first jump, a big box of white rails filled with green juniper brush. Middie circled at the trot and gave Holiday the canter signal. He shot forward and raced between the red and white starting flags fluttering in the wind. Middie wondered, how did he know this was a speed class?

She was afraid to check him; if he argued with her, she'd lose time. I'll just try to steady him and hope he doesn't cream a fence, Middie thought.

The girl leaned forward just the way Brian always did during a speed class. Holiday's heart pounded with the excitement of jumping at top speed. Brian had taught him how to race around the jumping course, spinning and cutting corners at every chance. He remembered the hush at each fence, and the yelling and cheering when he cleared it. Afterward, Brian always patted the

Leibergood

*horse's shoulder and said, "Good job, Magic!
You're great!" Now there was only silence each
time he landed. The horse doubled his effort.*

They cleared the big brush and when they
landed, Middie felt him bolt. He had been racing
like the wind before; what in heaven's name was
this? Was this what Mrs. Bailey had meant about
showing too soon? Holiday went over the second
fence, an oxer, and bulled into the bit, blasting
straight ahead. Middie used all her strength to
swing him in the direction of the third fence and
as they came barreling up to the vertical, she
checked him hard. At the last second he looked
at the fence, took off, and cleared the top rail by
a foot.

When he landed, Middie felt that his gallop was
much steadier, not so wild. Maybe he'd decided
that he'd better listen. Middie took heart.

There was a sharp turn before they could take
the brick wall. She sat up a little and used her
weight and legs to gather him up under her.

Holiday spun almost on his haunches and leapt
forward in response. Middie's courage rose with
the horse as they shot over the brick wall, still
clean.

He really was a great jumper, she thought. He's
done all this before, and he's remembering how
to take each fence. She thought of the oxer and
the triple bar and made her decision. Never mind
the S curve; she would jump the two fences as

though they were in a straight line.

She approached the oxer at an angle that lined up the triple bar beyond it as much as possible. She heard a gasp from the crowd as they realized what she was going to do. She collected the horse and built up his impulsion two strides from the fence and on the last stride, let him go. There was total silence in the grandstands as they cleared the oxer.

She laid her boots hard against the horse when they landed, and he leapt toward the triple bar at an angle. In two big strides the horse was there, and then Middie felt as though they were flying ten miles up in the air. She knew it was a miracle she was still with him when he landed. The roar of approval from the crowd was almost deafening.

They took the Garden Gate fence easily, and as she headed for the stone wall she heard the crowd gasp and groan. As they flew over the fence, she suddenly realized what had happened and her heart felt like it had turned to stone. In a daze she heard the whistle blow.

She had taken the wrong fence. She was off course, and she was eliminated.

She couldn't believe it. Holiday fought to keep going, but she circled him and brought him to a stop amid moans from the crowd. He tossed his head as they trotted out of the ring to applause, but everything was blurred through her tears. How could she do such a thing? How could she make such a stupid mistake, just as she had the class won? Middie leaned over and draped her arms around the sweaty neck. "Oh, I'm sorry, Holiday, I'm so sorry!" she exclaimed. "You were wonderful, and I let you down!"

Susie ran up to her. "Oh, Middie, how awful. You would have won the class easily. What a jump you made! Everyone is talking about it."

Middie shook her head. "I don't know what happened. I guess I was just so excited over taking the oxer and triple."

When the awards for the class were made, Mike rode out of the ring carrying a large silver tray and a set of long blue ribbons with gold letters.

Middie's family was waiting for her.

"Why did you go off course?" asked Laurie. "I thought you knew which fences to take."

Janet said quickly, "Anybody can go off course. I've seen it happen before." She looked defiantly at Laurie, and Middie wanted to cheer.

Her mother said, "You scared us to death with that one jump, but thank heavens you made it. I can't understand why you took the wrong fence."

"Neither can I," said Middie sadly. She didn't want to look at Mrs. Bailey.

"I can tell you," said Mrs. Bailey. "It's easy to go off course when you're concentrating so hard on one fence. Each time you land, you must think two fences ahead. That's why I asked you to go back and look at the whole course." She shrugged and smiled. "But the way you took the oxer and triple bar was excellent. You decided to trust him."

Laurie said in an exasperated voice, "You mean you went off course because you didn't take time to go back and look?"

Mrs. Bailey shook her head. "No. Sometimes riders go off course no matter how often they've walked it. It's hard to imagine the pressure when you're riding that fast."

Middie wiped her face on her jacket sleeve. She looked at Mrs. Bailey. "You knew," said Middie, trying to smile. "You said he could do it."

"I'm proud of the way you rode that combination."

Janet said grandly, "So am I!"

Middie's father cleared his throat. "I didn't know they made horses with rocket engines. That was quite a ride." His voice sounded funny.

"But she's eliminated!" said Laurie. "After all that, she blew it."

Their father smiled at Middie. " I think we can call it a learning experience. You and that horse are quite a pair."

Middie bit her lip and turned Holiday away to walk and cool him out. It was her own fault. She should have gone back and looked again at the fences. When would she ever learn?

She was entered in one more class, the Working Hunters Cross-Country. She still had one more chance to win, or at least get a ribbon. Now she knew she could count on Holiday and his tremendous jumping ability. It was up to her. She put her chin up with determination. She would ride better than she ever had before.

She went back to the trailer to dismount and looked up to see Mike Mitchell walking toward her, leading Jiffy. She turned away and busied herself with her saddle. She didn't want to see him. She had made such a dumb mistake in front of everybody!

"You sure came close to beating me!" Mike exclaimed. "That oxer and triple bar was a humongous combination, and you took it beautifully." He looked at her with admiration.

Middie shook her head. "I was scared at first to try it, but after your round, that was my only chance to win. And then I blew it all by going off course."

"Yeah, that can happen." He grinned. "I thought about lining up those two fences, but I decided not to take the chance. Jiffy isn't quite up to that big a jump. I didn't think any other horse was, either." He laughed ruefully. "You've got some horse."

"He is a great jumper," agreed Middie. Her face clouded. "Except for a ditch. There's a ravine in the canyon where I ride, and he won't go near it. I've tried and tried, but he starts sweating and shaking, so I've had to give it up. I don't know if he'll jump any other ditch. I think he might have fallen into something like that once and gotten hurt, and he won't forget it."

Mike shook his head. "From the way he took that last class, you'll soon have him taking every ditch jump. He sure has the ability. Just hang in there, and be patient."

"I need more than patience," she said. "He needs a better rider than me to get him over a ditch."

Mike's eyebrows shot up. "A better rider?"

"Somebody like you," said Middie. "I wish you would ride him."

"*Me!*" He shook his head. "You don't need anyone else to school him; you're doing fine. How old is he?"

"Maybe twenty or so."

Mike's mouth dropped open. "You've got to be kidding."

"I'm not kidding. We don't know who he is, or who used to own him. He came from the Pomona auction, and I named him Happy Holiday. I'm sure he used to be a really great horse."

"You may be right. Looks like Jiffy has some stiff competition."

Middie grinned. "I hope so. We're in the Working Hunters Cross-Country next."

"Well, whaddya know. So am I."

Susie had come over. "I'm in it, too. Let's go look at the course." Her round face became serious. "Say, if this is your first time here, you haven't seen the water jump. It's the sixth fence in Working Hunters."

"A water jump!" Middie stiffened. "What's *that* like?"

"It's really a splash jump," explained Mike. "There's a two-foot-drop bank, and then the water, about a foot deep and maybe twenty feet long, with a three-foot fence at the end of it."

Middie's face showed disbelief. "How can a horse possibly jump all that?"

"He doesn't," said Susie. "You jump in and gallop through and jump out over the fence. Let's go look."

They walked to the edge of the hunt field, and Susie pointed to a group of people gathered at some sort of obstacle.

"That's where it is. There's always a big crowd because so many riders fall off. Sometimes when the horse gets a good look at the water he stops, but the rider keeps on going."

"Good grief! I don't want to try that. Holiday has jumped over streams, but I've never asked him to jump into water."

Susie looked at her with sympathy. "If I'd known that, I would have kept my big mouth shut."

"Don't worry," Mike declared. "I'll bet your horse has been through a hundred splash jumps."

"Do you think so?"

"Sure. The splash jump won't be a problem for you." He grinned. "But you'd better be prepared for the eighth fence. It's a ditch."

"Oh, no!" Middie's heart missed a couple of beats and sank. She felt sick. "Let's go back. I've got to tell Mrs. Bailey."

18.
The Ditch Jump

Middie's family and Janet and Mrs. Bailey were gathered around the tailgate of their station wagon. A bright red-checked tablecloth was spread over the tailgate, and on it were baskets of various chips and some garlic bread, a bowl of potato salad, a huge container of fried chicken, and a big pan of chocolate-frosted brownies. Mrs. Bailey was helping herself to the chicken when Middie and Susie hurried back from the hunt field.

"Oh, Mrs. Bailey," blurted out Middie. "You should see the Working Hunter course! There's a huge splash jump after an Irish bank for the sixth fence, and the eighth one is a ditch. I shouldn't have entered!"

"Balderdash!" exclaimed Mrs. Bailey. "You told me you were tired of taking the same old fences. You rode very well in the Fault and Out. Why stop now?" She turned to Susie. "Do have lunch with us. We have enough food for an army."

Middie stared at Mrs. Bailey. "What if Holiday refuses the splash jump?"

"You'll probably get wet," she said, "but you'll dry out. Susie, there's potato salad, fried chicken, and brownies. How about it?"

Susie's face lit up. "All my favorites. How can I say no? Mom expected me to buy a hot dog."

"Fine. Take a paper plate and help yourself. There's lemonade and soft drinks over there."

Janet said quickly to Middie, "You know Holiday will refuse that ditch jump even if you do get through the splash. I don't want you to get hurt. Please scratch — it's not too late. I'll go with you to the office."

The idea that an old lady was urging her to take a chance, and a girl her own age wanted her to quit, struck Middie as funny. She laughed. "Not me. Cross-country is too much fun."

Mrs. Bailey smiled. "That's the spirit. Come and have lunch."

Janet stared at Middie. A little frown puckered her forehead and then suddenly cleared. "You won't win anything with Holiday, but I have an idea. I'll tell you later."

The food looked delicious, but after Middie had filled her plate her throat suddenly had a big lump. She put her plate down and moved her chair beside Mrs. Bailey's under the oak trees. She couldn't play games with Mrs. Bailey.

"I'm scared."

"That's not surprising. That's a big course. But I think you can do it."

"Can Holiday take that ditch jump?"

"Of course, he can. If he wants to." Mrs. Bailey looked thoughtfully at the drumstick in her hand. "Wanting to depends on how much he trusts you. He'll never forget the terrible thing that happened to him, but he has more confidence in you every day. If you could have waited a little longer . . ."

Middie squirmed. "Well, I couldn't."

"I don't recall anyone else taking the oxer and the triple bar like you did this morning." Mrs. Bailey sounded proud.

"That's true, isn't it?" Middie glowed at the unexpected praise. "Holiday sure can jump."

"Yes, he can. And he trusts you more each day." She looked Middie square in the eye. "If you're going to ride at all, then ride to take every jump."

Middie studied her boots for a minute and then smiled. "Thanks, Mrs. Bailey. I'll ride." The fried chicken tasted pretty good after all.

After lunch Middie and Susie rode to the warm-up ring to wait for the call for Working Hunters. Susie was the tenth to ride. Middie wished her luck and tried to keep her thoughts on Holiday.

After a long interval Susie returned triumphantly, her round face pink and shining. "I made it! I had a really good go," she told Middie excitedly. "Lucky Buck didn't slow up once or refuse anything. If only he were like that in the ring!"

One by one the riders returned, their stirrups up, leading their horses. Two of them were soaking wet and crying. A couple more looked really mad, and one of the boys was saying some interesting words that Middie had never heard before. She shut her eyes and tried to recall the thrill she had felt going over the triple bar. Holiday had trusted her. He hadn't hesitated a second.

The loudspeaker announced Middie's number. She licked her dry lips, tried to keep her hands steady, and trotted Holiday out into the field to the starting flags.

The horse broke to a gallop, picked up speed, and charged toward the red and white flags framing the first obstacle. He took the first fence easily and in stride. As soon as he landed, he settled into a pace so steady that Middie wasn't frightened, even when the scenery began to blur. There was plenty of room between fences to make the turns, and Holiday was watching where he was going. Middie leaned into the wind over his neck and rejoiced at the powerful strides that carried her.

The flags and the jumps and the rolling country triggered a hundred memories for Holiday. He raced boldly, joyfully, over the cross-country course, recognizing each kind of obstacle although he had never seen that particular one before. Even when the girl was uncertain about a fence, she brought him in at a good angle and then let him figure out the best way to take it.

They flew over one obstacle after another so smoothly, Middie hardly felt them. They cleared the big barrels, sailed over the snake fence at the highest level, took the cord of wood, and turned for the splash jump.

Middie felt the horse tense briefly when he saw the glitter of sunlight on the water, but he did not slow down. He took off smoothly and landed way out in the water with walls of spray far above her head. In two strides they were through, and then out and over the fence at the far end. It was so beautiful that Middie could have cried for joy. She patted his shoulder and shouted, "Good boy!"

They took the post and rail easily, and Middie turned him down the slope for the ditch.

She drove him hard like she had at the triple bar, commanding him with her whole body. The ditch yawned black and wide.

Just as they reached the ditch, the horse stiffened, skidded a few feet, and spun to the right.

He just couldn't help it. All the exciting days of galloping and jumping fearlessly across the country with Brian vanished when he saw the ditch. Into his memory flashed the one time he had been ridden by the other boy, the one they called Darryl, when Darryl took him at a dead run across the rolling desert country where the awful ravine lay, half-hidden by the sagebrush. The memory of what had happened next swept over Holiday and in terror he spun away.

Middie flew over the ditch without him and rolled down the slope. She scrambled to her feet, unhurt, and looked around.

Holiday stood near the ditch, head down, reins trailing, and sweat pouring from his shaking body.

People began running toward them.

"Let him alone!" Middie called out. She walked around the obstacle and took hold of his reins. Her eyes stung with tears of frustration. "Easy, boy, easy," she said, stroking the shivering horse. He leaned against her.

Her parents hurried out to meet her.

"Middie, oh, Middie!" exclaimed her mother. "What an awful fall! Did you break anything?"

"No, I'm okay." She ran up her stirrups and began to lead Holiday away.

"Are you sure?" asked her father, falling into step beside her. "You're not hurt?"

"Not a bit," said Middie. For once, he hadn't made a joke. "Yes, I hurt my pride." She smiled. "I'll see you later — I have to get Holiday off the course."

Susie and Mike were waiting for her at the gate.

"Are you really okay?" asked Susie.

Middie nodded and brushed the dirt from her breeches.

Mike said, "Well, now you know he doesn't like *any* kind of a ditch. You weren't kidding about his not liking that ravine, were you? I was sure he'd take the ditch after the way he jumped everything else."

"So was I." She stood up and straightened her hunt cap. "I guess nobody would want to ride him at a ditch jump after that."

Mike smiled. "That's a real challenge. He *is* a super jumper." His face turned serious. "If you're sure you want me to ride him, I wouldn't mind having a crack at it."

"You *will* ride him?" Middie glowed. "Oh, Mike, I'm sure you can make him jump it!"

"Well, I'll try. I'll ask for permission to school in the hunt field as soon as it's clear." Mike whistled cheerfully as he rode off on Jiffy for his turn.

19.
A Stomachache

Middie watched Mike's big bay horse gallop over the course, arching his body and folding his front legs carefully over every fence. If only Holiday would jump a cross-country course like that!

No one was surprised when Mike rode out of the ring at the end of the class with Jiffy wearing a blue ribbon on his bridle and Mike carrying another silver platter.

Susie was bouncing up and down in her saddle. "I got a fourth! I got a fourth!" she chanted, and Middie pinned the white ribbons on Lucky Buck's bridle for everyone to see.

"Guess what!" Middie said to Mrs. Bailey. "Mike Mitchell is going to school Holiday over the ditch jump when they've cleared the course."

"*What?*" Mrs. Bailey's gray eyes flashed. "You're letting someone else ride Holiday?"

"Well, yes, but Mike isn't just anybody. He's a supergood rider."

"Why in the world do you want someone else

to ride that horse?" Mrs. Bailey's cane fiercely punched little holes in the grass. "It seems to me you'd want to take your time and do it yourself."

"I'm not good enough. Once Mike jumps Holiday over the ditch, I can make him do it, too. I can't keep riding a horse that won't ever jump a ditch in working hunters. I'll always be eliminated." She looked around. "Where's Janet? What did she think of the cross-country?"

"She's lying down in the back of the station wagon. She got a stomachache just before the cross-country started."

"She didn't even *see* the cross-country? She didn't see Holiday take all those fences and the splash jump?"

"No." Mrs. Bailey stood up slowly. Middie thought she looked tired. "Why don't you find her and tell her you're all right?"

"All right?" asked Middie blankly. "Oh, she probably thought I was going to get hurt." She made a face. "I suppose she said she and Minaret could easily have taken the whole course."

Mrs. Bailey smiled. "Something like that."

"Her horse can do everything," exclaimed Middie, "but she can't even watch the cross-country class! What kind of a rider is she, anyway?"

A vague suspicion floating in the back of Middie's mind in a fog suddenly loomed in front of her and took shape, sharply defined. She drew a deep breath.

"I wonder if Janet is making up a lot of that

stuff about winning all those shows. Sure, she had a pony. But I don't see how she can ride a horse like Minaret when she doesn't know how to handle horses!"

"That's possible, but I wouldn't . . ."

"Possible!" exploded Middie. "She brags all the time about Minaret, but she's scared to death of horses. Did you see how scared she is of Holiday? Maybe Minaret isn't even a real horse."

Mrs. Bailey's face clouded. "She's afraid of Holiday, yes. She's afraid of a lot of things. Right now, she's afraid something happened to you in the cross-country."

Middie said, "Oh." She wished she hadn't said all those things about Janet to Mrs. Bailey, even if she really felt like that sometimes. Janet was still her friend, no matter what weird ideas she had about horses and riding.

Janet really cares what happens to me, thought Middie.

"I'll go see her," Middie said. She went to the station wagon and peered into the back. Janet was lying down with her face in a pillow. "Hey, Jan, I'm sorry you feel bad."

Janet rolled over and sat up. "Is the cross-country over? Are you okay?"

"Yeah, it's over. You sure missed a good class."

Janet opened the car door. "What happened?"

"Mike won." Middie gave a quick laugh. "Holiday and I were just great till we got to the ditch jump. Then he froze, and I took the ditch all by myself. I'm getting good at that."

"You're sure you weren't hurt?" Janet climbed out and looked at her friend closely.

Middie shook her head. "Not a bit."

Janet's face brightened. "I'm glad." She twisted a lock of hair around her finger. "I'm awfully sorry you fell off, but that's just what I expected. That horse will never be reliable."

Janet might be right, but Middie wasn't going to admit it. Instead, she asked, "Want to see some excitement? Mike Mitchell is going to ride Holiday for me. When the classes in the hunt field are over, Mike is going to take Holiday over the ditch."

Janet's mouth dropped open. "That's crazy! I don't want to watch him try. I hate to see an accident."

"Mike won't get hurt. He's a great rider. Everybody's going. You come, too."

Janet was quiet for a minute. "Well, all right, I'll come with you. I just hope nothing terrible happens. When somebody gets hurt, I throw up."

Middie put her arm around Janet's shoulders and gave her a hug. "Nobody's going to get hurt."

As soon as the last cross-country class was over, they all set out for the hunt field. Middie led Holiday and made him walk slowly so Mrs. Bailey could keep up. Janet walked beside Middie's parents, talking earnestly.

She's probably telling them *she*'s never fallen

off, and she and Minaret could have won that class, thought Middie. They'll believe her, too.

Middie sighed. Thank goodness Mike was going to ride Holiday. After that, things would be different.

20.
Holiday Attacks

Mike met them with a cheerful grin. "I put Jiffy in his trailer so I could concentrate on Holiday. I'll use my own saddle." He motioned to the nearby rail.

Middie stripped Holiday and put her saddle on the rail next to Mike's. She rubbed Holiday's neck in back of his jaw for reassurance and whispered, "You're going to have a super-rider on you now. Show him how good you really are."

Mike lifted his saddle from the rail and walked up to Holiday.

When Holiday saw the boy with the saddle walk toward him, he suddenly remembered the other boy who had galloped with him across the high desert, jumping chaparral and rocks and little gullies, just as he used to gallop with Brian.

He remembered the smell of sage and the hot summer wind in his face as they galloped. The boy on his back was so light, he had hardly felt him at all, and his hooves had thundered over the

139

hard-packed ground. Ahead of them yawned a huge ravine, and the horse had eagerly lengthened his stride and then launched himself into space over the dark chasm.

He remembered in midair the scream of terror from the boy, and he had suddenly felt a frightful jerk of the reins that twisted his head around and pulled him down. Instead of the prairie on the far side, the clay banks and dry rocks of the riverbed below came rushing up to meet him. Holiday remembered the frightful crash, and then nothing at all.

Middie saw the horse stiffen with fear.

Just as Mike swung the saddle, the thoroughbred's ears flattened. He trumpeted, reared up to his full height, and drove his powerful forelegs at the boy.

Mike yelled and half-fell, half-leaped backward, and the iron-shod hooves flashed just past his head. Again, Holiday trumpeted and rose on his hind legs, his nostrils flaring with hatred.

Mike dropped his saddle and vaulted over the fence. Janet screamed and scrambled over the fence to join him. She sprawled on the grass, looking like she might be sick.

Middie shouted, "No! Holiday, NO!" People screamed and shouted and ran. Middie grabbed wildly for Holiday's reins, yelling, "Keep quiet, everybody! Keep quiet!" She finally got hold of the reins and dragged the trembling horse away. He was still blowing fiercely through his nostrils as Middie tried to calm him.

"What happened?" Mike exclaimed. "I've never even seen that horse before!" His freckles stood out like polka dots on his white face.

Mrs. Bailey's face was just as white. "I'm sure you haven't, Mike, but you obviously remind him of someone he hates dreadfully. Thank heavens you got out of his way."

Mike swung his saddle onto the rail and collapsed on the grass. "That was too close for comfort!"

Middie, with trembling fingers, tied Holiday to a tree and rejoined them. "He's *never* acted like that before!"

"Never had me start to get on him, either," said Mike. He tried to grin, but it came out lopsided. "Have you had any trouble with him?"

Middie shook her head, bewildered. "He's been just fine with me."

"It's a boy he's afraid of," said Mrs. Bailey. "A boy who rode him or handled him, and did something that Holiday will never forget."

"Now we know why a horse with that much talent ended up in the auction," said Mike. "I'm not chicken, but I know when to quit. He's got too big a problem."

As Mike stood up, he saw the stricken look on Middie's face. He tilted his hunt cap sideways and made a funny face. "I want Mom and Dad to meet you. They won't believe there's a kid who rides a horse that I can't ride."

Middie smiled faintly. "Thanks for trying to ride him. I'm awfully sorry about what happened."

"So am I." He shrugged. "Forget it. I want you to visit our thoroughbred farm. It's called Highgate Hills, and we have a couple hundred horses out there you can look at."

"I'd like that very much," said Middie.

Mike slung his saddle over one arm. "I'll ask Mom to phone you and make it official."

The subdued group returned to the horse trailer and began packing up. Holiday was still nervous and jumped and blew at every little clump of grass.

Janet joined her at the trailer, standing a respectful distance from the horse. "That horse is a terror. Didn't I tell you so from the beginning?"

Middie said nothing. She threw the blanket over Holiday and fumbled with the buckles.

"At least your parents have some sense," Janet said.

Middie straightened up. "What about my parents?"

Janet twisted her fingers and looked away. "I was just talking to them, that's all. It's part of my plan to have them get you a better horse." She turned and walked toward the refreshment stand.

Middie caught up with her. "What did you say?" asked Middie.

"I told them you were a really good rider, and you ought to have a really good horse."

"Thanks." Middie hesitated. "What else?"

Janet shrugged. "Nothing much."

"Tell me," demanded Middie. "You'd better tell me."

Janet took a deep breath. "I said Holiday is dangerous, and you shouldn't be riding him, and that's the truth."

"You told them that?" yelled Middie. "What kind of a friend are you? That's the only horse I can enter in shows, and you want me to give him up?"

"It's a good thing they saw for themselves what he's really like." Janet shook her head. "They're going to make you quit riding him."

"Quit riding him!" shrieked Middie. "I thought you were my friend! I *hate* you!"

"Don't yell like that. I *am* your friend." Her voice was pleading. "I don't want you hurt. I even wrote my trainer to have some friends of his out here look for a *good* horse for you. I'll talk your family into it."

"Don't you understand?" shouted Middie. "My family can't afford it. They won't *ever* get me a horse! I can't stop riding Holiday. He's the only horse I've got that I can show."

"Well, you haven't *got* Holiday. He belongs to

143

Halsey, and Halsey's going to sell him."

Middie groaned. "But I want to ride him until he's sold. If you don't fix it with Mom and Dad for me to ride him, I'll never speak to you again. *Ever!*"

Janet eyes filled with tears. "But you'll get hurt really bad if you keep on riding that horse." There was a long silence. Middie stared back grimly until Janet dropped her eyes. Middie turned and stamped back to the horse trailer.

She leaned against Holiday. She suddenly realized how much she loved him, even though he was deaf, even though he was difficult to ride. She snapped her mind shut and refused to think about his being sold. Mrs. Bailey must somehow get her parents to let her keep on riding him. Tears welled up in her eyes and spilled down her cheeks. How do you make a horse forget?

21.
Decisions, Decisions

"Just because Mrs. Bailey says Holiday can teach you a lot doesn't make him any safer to ride," insisted Janet. "I just wish she hadn't talked your parents into letting you keep on riding him after what he did at the horse show."

Nearly three weeks had passed since the show. Janet was sitting on the bench in the barnyard watching Middie brush the big chestnut horse. His copper coat gleamed in the sunlight.

Middie stepped back to admire him. "He's never tried to hurt *me*. Besides, I'd rather ride Holiday than any other horse."

Janet scuffed the dirt with one tennis shoe and shook her head. "I was sure your folks were going to get you a good horse. I was working on it. Now you're stuck with crazy old Holiday."

"He's *not* crazy," Middie declared. "And how many times do I have to tell you my folks don't have enough money to buy me a horse, even if your trainer did know somebody out here, which he doesn't." She lifted the saddle onto his back.

"But your favorite classes are cross-country jumping, and there are always ditches. Nobody will think you're a good rider if you get dumped into every ditch. You've got to have a horse you can win with."

Middie didn't say anything. She smoothed out the saddle pad and began buckling the girth.

Janet sighed. "I might as well change the jumps for you. Mrs. Bailey wants you to work on combinations today."

Middie brightened. Once in a while Janet gave her a pain, but the rest of the time she was really nice to have around. How fast the summer had gone. Middie would sure miss her when she went back home to Connecticut next week.

A truck rumbled into the area in back of the barn. It coughed and hiccuped like Halsey's pickup. Middie swung up into the saddle. Halsey had been terribly disappointed at the horse show. If it was Halsey, she could show him how much both she and the horse had improved since then.

It was Halsey. He clomped down the hill to the barn, tipped back his hat from his leathery face, and squinted up at the thoroughbred. "How is that big horse comin' along?"

"We're doing pretty well. He doesn't argue much anymore. See how he holds his head? Doesn't he look elegant?"

Halsey nodded and leaned on the rail, his blue eyes fixed on horse and rider.

Holiday seemed to know he was being watched.

He arched his neck and played gently with the bit, snorting softly under his breath. Middie guided him through circles and serpentines and figure eights.

Several times Middie glanced at Halsey's face. He was watching, but he didn't show any feelings. What was wrong? He ought to be happy with the way Holiday was going.

She turned the thoroughbred toward one of the fences. He often began rushing, but today he jumped like an old hunter. Middie finished with a big fence of poles and barrels. She brought the horse to a halt, backed five steps, and rode over to Halsey.

"What do you think of *that*?" she asked triumphantly.

"I'll see you when you've put him away."

Not a word of approval! Middie watched him join Mrs. Bailey on the front porch. They sat down, talking seriously. What was going on?

Middie cooled out the horse and dismounted. She was leading Holiday back to the barn when Janet fell into step beside her.

"Did you see Halsey's truck?" she asked. "He's got the horse trailer hitched on. It's empty."

Middie's heart lurched. "So?"

"So maybe he's sold Holiday and he's come to take him away. That would be a good thing, too."

Middie scowled at her. "I hope you're wrong."

Janet shook her head sadly and walked slowly back to the house.

Middie sponged off the saddle marks on Holiday's back and scraped him carefully. If Halsey was going to take Holiday away, wouldn't he have just told her?

She put her cheek against the copper neck. Holiday turned his head and gave her a friendly shove.

"Middie, would you come here?" called Mrs. Bailey.

Middie dropped the scraper as if she had been scalded and ran up the steps. Janet was leaning against the railing of the top step, looking glum, and Mrs. Bailey and Halsey were sitting on the porch chairs, Halsey with his boots on the railing.

"What is it?" Middie asked. Their faces were solemn. "Can I . . . do something for you?"

"Well, now, that all depends." Halsey smiled, almost mournfully. "You been ridin' that hunk o' horseflesh okay."

She cleared her throat. "Thanks, Halsey."

"He sure ain't Rusty, but ain't no way I can prove it, even if I found out where he came from. Which I can't." He paused. "Who cares? Seems like I got me a real good jumper instead of some kid's horse."

Middie's heart was beating painfully. "Have you found somebody who wants Holiday?"

Halsey met her gaze directly. "Yup. I found somebody who sure would like him."

"Are they going to buy him?"

148

Halsey stretched out his legs and studied his boots. "I dunno. They don't know all there is to know about that old horse."

Middie tried to keep her voice steady. "I suppose you want me to ride him so they can see what he's like?"

Halsey ignored her question. "For one thing, that horse is nearly deaf."

Mrs. Bailey drew in her breath sharply. There was a small silence.

Middie said in a calm voice, "I knew that."

The others looked startled.

Mrs. Bailey said, "You *what*?"

"I knew that. I found it out the day I had my first lesson on him. He had his head down inside the barrel of A and M when I went to catch him. I was talking all the time, but when I touched him, he jumped and whirled."

"And you never said a word!" Mrs. Bailey exclaimed.

"I thought about it. And then I decided I wanted to see how well I could ride him even though he couldn't hear any voice commands." She tilted up her chin. "Nobody could tell except me." She looked at Halsey. "When did you find out?"

Halsey frowned. "I thought somethin' might be wrong when we was at the horse show. After you went off course, and the judge blew his whistle, that horse kept right on goin' as though he hadn't heard the whistle a-tall. A horse with that many miles on him would prob'ly know the signal."

"Holiday just likes to keep going," Middie pointed out.

"And goin' back to the trailer, we went right by a horse van with a big ruckus goin' on inside, with a horse squealin' and bangin' and people yellin'. If he'd a-heard that, he woulda been upset, but he didn't pay no attention."

"I remember the van," said Mrs. Bailey. "How deaf is he?"

Middie shook her head. "At first I thought he was completely deaf, but now sometimes I think he can hear a little bit. I'm not sure. I wonder how it happened?"

"Prob'ly got a crack on the head, maybe the time he was messed up at the ditch."

"That explains why he wouldn't lunge," said Mrs. Bailey. "It explains a lot of things."

Middie said, "But the people that want him, how will they feel when they find out he's practically deaf?"

"I dunno," said Halsey. "How do *you* feel?"

"It doesn't make any difference to *me*!" she declared. "I was careful he always saw me before I touched him. I told him I would be his ears, and he would be everything else for me. Look how well we've gotten along together."

Halsey nodded solemnly. "That's what I was hoping you'd say. Girl, I'll tell you, finding a good home for a horse like that ain't the easiest thing in the world. Seein' as how you like him so much, I druther give him to you than try to sell him someplace where he wouldn't be treated right."

Middie's heart skidded to a halt. *"Give* him to *me?"*

Halsey smiled for the first time. "You might say somethin' besides just repeatin' what I said. Whyn't you say yes?"

Middie stared at him, and suddenly her heart made a big jump and was beating again. Holiday could be hers? *Her own horse?* She wanted to yell and sing and dance. She was about to leap out of her chair with a war whoop when Mrs. Bailey spoke up.

"This is something you'll want to think over very carefully, Middie. Getting a horse isn't like getting a bicycle or a stereo. It's a new member of your family."

"Yes, but I've always wanted a . . ."

"There are quite a few other things to consider," Mrs. Bailey went on. "Holiday is old. You'll have only three or four more years of riding him, and then he'll have to be retired."

"I don't have to think about that now."

"Yes, you do. Of course you can keep him here. And you should know I'm willing to let him stay on when he's retired, even after you get another horse. Derry isn't going to last forever, and I'd be lost without an old horse around the place to keep me company."

Middie was bewildered. How could Mrs. Bailey possibly think about Holiday getting too old to be ridden, or think about Derry dying, when right this minute Halsey was offering Middie a horse of her own?

"And another thing," Mrs. Bailey went on. "Holiday is going to take a lot of time and effort. This is something you can't rush through. He may never take a ditch jump for you, either, no matter how much work you put into him."

Halsey nodded. "Mizz Bailey is right, Middie. It's something you got to think over. I know you love that horse, and he'd have a good home, but you got to think of all the angles."

"I should hope so!" exclaimed Janet. "Holiday isn't really the right horse for you. You need a horse you can win with, not get eliminated with half the time."

Mrs. Bailey interrupted. "The decision is Middie's. Let her make up her own mind. If she has time to think it through, I'm sure she'll come to the right decision . . . what's right for her, as well as what's right for the horse."

"I . . . I don't know what to say," Middie stammered. "I sure do thank you, Halsey. I . . . I guess I should think about it for a while." What Janet and Mrs. Bailey had said disturbed her. Riding Holiday for fun was one thing, but having a horse with that kind of handicap for keeps?

"How soon do you want to know?" she asked.

Halsey shrugged. "Take your time. I ain't in no hurry. There's a horse auction almost every week someplace."

Janet shook her head sadly. "I wish there were some way to get you a good horse."

Middie said, "What do you suppose my folks will say?"

Mrs. Bailey pursed her lips. "You'll have to talk it over with them. If you're certain you're making the right decision, I believe they'll go along with it. I think it will be up to you."

Middie was in a daze. To have a horse of her own right this minute . . . no more waiting and dreaming and saving. A beautiful horse, with such talent. Then uneasily she remembered the gully, the ditch jump, and Holiday's attack on Mike. She really *did* have a lot to think over.

Suddenly things that had been important weren't important at all. They were supposed to go to Mike Mitchell's farm, Highgate Hills, on Thursday with Janet and Mrs. Bailey. Now she didn't even want to go. She wanted to stay home and ride Holiday. She wanted to know what it was like to ride him if he was going to be her very own horse.

He was difficult to ride; so far, he'd only made Laurie disgusted with Middie's performance at the horse show. Making him forget his fears would take an awfully long time. And what if he never

did? If he never would jump a ditch, did she really
want that kind of a horse?

"You have a lot to think about, but keeping busy
will give your mind a chance to work," said Mrs.
Bailey, looking at Middie. She smiled as if she had
read Middie's mind. "Going to Highgate Hills will
help."

22.
Highgate Hills Farm

Davie and Laurie had been invited to Highgate
Hills Farm, too. Middie was surprised when
Laurie had said she and David would go with
them. Probably their mom had made her say yes
so they could go in David's car. Mrs. Bailey never
drove on the freeways.

The morning of the big excursion Middie lin-
gered over Holiday. "I just wish I knew what was
the right thing to do," she told the horse as she
cleaned his stall. "I'd love for you to be mine, but
you'd have to change a lot for Mom and Dad to
be impressed." She sighed deeply. "You don't
know what it's like hearing them make a fuss over
Laurie all the time. They're never satisfied with
what I do." She wiped her face on her sleeve.

"You know what? I'm going to ride you up the
canyon one of these days, and you're going to look
at that little gully. Someday you're going to jump
it."

She was finishing Derry's stall when David's car

155

pulled up the driveway. She saw Mrs. Bailey get in beside Janet in the backseat.

She waved and hurried to finish. Both horses had their heads deep in their mangers with breakfast. Middie couldn't resist going into Holiday's stall one more time to pat him. "You'd better get ready to look at that gully," she told him.

She washed up and raced to the car. She started to get in and then hesitated. She couldn't remember fastening the chain on Derry's paddock.

"Come *on*, Caboose," said Laurie.

Middie clamped her mouth shut. Laurie had ignored her since the horse show. Middie climbed in and slammed the car door. "I'm ready."

As soon as they left the city behind, the smog faded, and the sky shone brilliant blue. The silvergray ribbon of freeway looped over the amber hills, and the whole countryside seemed to shimmer in the late-summer sunlight. Middie wondered if it was really this beautiful, or if it was knowing she had been offered a horse that cast this special glow.

The entrance to Highgate Hills Farm was framed by ornate wrought-iron gates and a gate house. A uniformed guard stepped out to meet them.

"Middie Scott to see Mike Mitchell," said Mrs. Bailey. The guard waved them through, and they started up the long driveway. On both sides of the road, herds of beautiful horses grazed on the hillsides, silhouetted darkly against the pale gold grass. Middie stared at the horses and wondered what it would be like to own a horse like one of those. She could say yes at any minute and have a beautiful horse of her own. Was she sure that was what she wanted?

They drove between two rows of tall palm trees to a long low ranch house with a tiled roof and a spacious courtyard in front. Behind the house were several large barns, and behind the barns, miles of paddocks and horses.

Mike and his mother were waiting for them in the shade of the courtyard. Mike grinned as they got out of the car. He looked very much like his mother — her hair was reddish and windblown, and her face, like his, was covered with freckles.

She smiled warmly as Mrs. Bailey introduced them. "How nice of you to come," she said. "Hello, Middie. I've heard so much about you and your riding, and that exciting horse of yours. And Janet. Janet Willoughby?" She looked thoughtful.

Janet turned a little pink. "I'm just visiting for the summer. I live back East."

Mrs. Mitchell nodded. "We'll have something cold to drink after your long drive; then we'll go sightseeing."

She offered them frosty glasses of lemonade out on the patio. Middie was polite and sat still to finish off her glass, but she could hardly wait to see the farm. She glanced at Mike and saw that he was eager, too. He waggled his eyebrows and winked solemnly like he had done at the show.

"There's so much to show you. Let's get going," Mike said at last. "We'll use the golf cart to drive around."

David and Laurie set off walking, holding hands, but the rest climbed into the cart.

They drove from barns to paddocks to fields, Middie keeping up a running "oh" and "wow" with great enthusiasm. "It's pretty nice," agreed Janet, which from her was a lot of praise.

Across from the riding ring where Mike trained his hunters was a large paddock with a handsome dark bay horse. The horse watched them come up to the fence. When Mike whistled, the horse trotted to meet them.

Middie patted his nose. The brass nameplate on his halter read, HASTY EXIT.

"He's gorgeous!" exclaimed Middie. "Does he race, too?"

Mike laughed. "Don't you recognize him? That's the horse I rode in the show where I met you, the horse we call Jiffy. Years ago my dad trained him and sold him as a jumper. He's sixteen years old and he's still great."

"I know," said Middie. "I saw all your blue ribbons."

"We had bought him back just before the show. Mom can't stand to see a horse not treated right, especially a horse that we raised. We're going to be real careful about his next owner. His last owner was a . . . well . . ." He let his voice trail off.

"Jiffy's sure lucky you got him back," said Middie. She stroked his neck. He nickered and dropped his head.

"We're terribly fond of that horse," Mrs. Mitchell said, smiling. "He's very well-trained. Would you like to ride him?"

"Right now?" exclaimed Middie. "Would I!"

"I'll go get a helmet for you," Mike said. "You'll want to jump him, and we're pretty particular about that."

One of the grooms saddled the big bay, and Middie scrambled up and rode him into the ring, just as Laurie and David caught up with them. The horse was full of energy, but he responded quickly to her commands. Middie tried different figures and then, because he was so smooth and easy to ride, she turned him to the first fence and took him over a short course. She pulled up in front of the group and shook her head in wonder.

"I've never ridden such a well-trained horse!"

"The rider has something to do with it," said Mrs. Mitchell. "You're as good a rider as Mike said you were."

Middie blushed. "Anybody could ride this horse; he's fantastic. What are you going to do with him?"

"Well," said Mike's mother, smiling broadly, "I'm hoping you would like to have him."

"Oh, no, Mrs. Mitchell. I couldn't afford a horse

like this. Besides, I've been offered . . ."

Mike interrupted her. "Mom wants to *give* you Jiffy, Middie. We want Jiffy to have a good home, and you deserve a better horse than that ex-steeplechaser you're riding."

23.
Middie Calls
a Bluff

Middie was stunned. She wanted to laugh and cry at the same time. From owning no horse at all, she had been offered two horses . . . free. Two absolutely beautiful horses.

She ran one hand over the sleek dark coat. "I don't know what to say," she said in a small voice. Jiffy tossed his head and looked around at her.

Mrs. Bailey planted her cane firmly on the ground and straightened up. "Middie has been offered the other horse, Holiday. She's been thinking about that."

"For goodness' sake," said Mrs. Mitchell. "Well, I shouldn't think that would be a hard decision to make. Mike tells me that Holiday is talented, but he'll never be a good show horse. You deserve something much better."

"You'll have a fantastic time with Jiffy," said Mike. "He takes every kind of jump there is, especially ditches."

Middie felt light-headed. To own Jiffy, that gorgeous horse she had seen Mike ride at Val Verde!

Laurie looked at her with real respect. She said, "They're *giving* you that beautiful horse we saw at the show?"

Middie nodded, and she heard David whistle in surprise.

"Jiffy's an excellent hunter," Mrs. Mitchell added. "He'll always take good care of you." Her eyes were bright. "I'll see that you have an invitation to ride on opening day of the Happy Valley Hunt Club. There's no fox, just a trail laid for the hounds to follow, but it will be exciting."

Middie stroked the big bay horse. She had been so happy over being offered Holiday, she was almost ready to say yes to Mr. Halsey. Then as Mrs. Bailey talked, Middie realized it wasn't that simple. She had begun to think of Holiday's problems, and how long it would take her to work on them.

And, oh, to own Jiffy! With Jiffy, she could win almost every show she took him in. . . . Why, she could even enter him at Idlewood. *Idlewood!* Her family would be proud of her.

"Mrs. Mitchell, I sure do thank you for thinking of me for Jiffy. He's an absolutely super horse." She looked at Mrs. Bailey. "Is this a dream, or is it for real?"

Everyone laughed, even Laurie.

"It's for real," said Mrs. Mitchell. "I'm sure you'll appreciate his ability. Why don't you ride him back to the ranch house? I'll have one of the grooms put him away for you afterward."

Middie rode beside the others in the little cart. Her heart was pounding, even though Jiffy was walking quietly. Jiffy would make possible her wildest dreams. She would never again be the Caboose; she would be an important member of the family.

She slid off the horse and ran the stirrups up. "I'll talk to my parents when we get home, and then I'll call you. Is that okay?"

"Certainly," said Mrs. Mitchell. "But you don't have to tell us right away. Owning a horse is a big decision. You could even wait until Saturday. You can phone me, and I'll arrange to have Jiffy trailered over on Sunday."

Janet pursed her lips. "I've been trying and trying to talk her parents into buying her a good horse, and now they won't have to. She'll love Jiffy. Thank goodness Halsey can get rid of that crazy Holiday."

Middie opened her mouth to make a sharp retort, but smiled instead. "You know a lot more about horses than I do, so you're probably right." She turned to Mrs. Mitchell. "Janet is an awfully good rider. She's won lots and lots of trophies on her horse, Silver Minaret."

"For goodness' sake!" said Mrs. Mitchell, looking at Janet with new interest.

Mrs. Bailey cleared her throat and looked sternly at Middie.

Middie plunged on. "Janet has told me lots about the horse shows she's won. She even won the Junior Championship at the Westchester Show this year."

"The Westchester Show?" said Mrs. Mitchell, startled. "I should have invited Janet to ride, too."

"It's not too late," said Middie with enthusiasm. "She could ride Jiffy around right now."

Janet stared at Middie. "No, thank you," she said. "I never ride without my trainer."

"Why not?" said Middie. "Mike's here, and he's a good trainer; you're a great rider. Isn't the Westchester Show one of the biggest, back East?"

"It certainly is," said Mrs. Mitchell. "I believe the last issue of the *Horse Chronicle* has the report about it."

Something clanged in Middie's head, and she felt a little dizzy. This was her chance to see if Janet was really making up all those horse show stories or not.

"Really?" said Middie, making her voice sound casual. "I'd love to see that!"

Mrs. Bailey set her lips in a straight line. Middie tried to smile back innocently.

Mrs. Mitchell disappeared into the house and returned shortly, leafing through the magazine she was carrying. "Why, here it is. Do look!" she said, holding out the page.

Middie looked. The photograph showed a girl on a beautiful, big gray hunter going over an enormous stone wall. The girl seemed to be in a trance — her face was pale and grim under her hunt cap. Middie gulped. She felt hot and cold. It was Janet.

The caption read, "Janet Willoughby on Silver Minaret, clinching the Junior Championship title at the Westchester Horse Show."

The words flew out before Middie could stop them. "Why, Janet, you really did!"

Everyone looked at Middie. She felt her face burn scarlet.

"What do you mean, 'you really did'?" asked Janet slowly.

If she lived to be 150 years old, Middie knew she would never forget that moment. She wished she were dead at the bottom of the ditch jump, dead, with everyone crowded around her, everyone sorry. Right now, nobody at all would be sorry.

She tried to hide her confusion. "I mean . . ." she stammered, ". . . you're always so scared . . . of Holiday!"

"I *told* you," said Janet, "that horse is *dangerous*. I know you think he's special, but you shouldn't be riding him."

"Oh," said Middie. Janet had always said that before, and Middie had ignored her. But the magazine page with Janet's image spread across it burned behind her eyes. Janet *was* a champion rider — and she had said Holiday was dangerous. She'd been saying it all summer. She knew what she was talking about. Middie felt dazed.

Janet was looking at Middie earnestly and saying something. Her words finally reached Middie as if from far away. "I think it's wonderful you can have Jiffy. He'll be the perfect horse for you."

24.
The Right Choice

Janet's voice echoed back and forth in Middie's head. The words rang true. Jiffy was indeed the perfect horse for her. Her family would *have* to be proud of her.

A wave of shame swept over Middie. She had practically called Janet a liar, but that hadn't kept Janet from saying what she thought was best for Middie. Janet was truly a best friend. With Jiffy, Middie could enter all the horse shows she wanted to — and win.

Middie said carefully, "Mrs. Mitchell, Janet is right. Jiffy will be a great horse for me. I'd be awfully proud to have him, and I'll take real good care of him. I . . . I'll never be able to thank you enough."

Mrs. Bailey's voice was cool. "And what about Holiday?"

Middie was surprised to find her throat aching. "I'll have to tell Halsey no thanks." She took a deep breath. "I love that horse, but Jiffy will be much better for me." She had a sudden thought. "But, Mike, who will you ride?"

He grinned broadly. "I have a young horse I'm just starting. In a couple more years, look out."

Everyone laughed. Mrs. Mitchell said, "I'm so glad you said yes. We'll have Jiffy brought over to Mrs. Bailey's on Sunday."

All the way home Middie sat quietly in a dream, while Janet and Mrs. Bailey talked horses and school and what Janet would do when she got back to Connecticut. Middie tried to picture the beautiful bay horse in the stall next to Derry. It wasn't easy; she kept seeing instead the chestnut thoroughbred. She brushed one arm across her face.

Maybe Derry would be friends with Jiffy. What a relief that would be. Derry had hated Holiday from the moment the thoroughbred came into the barn. Middie didn't know a horse could be so jealous.

As soon as her parents got home, she told them about Jiffy.

"Well, what a surprise!" exclaimed her mother. "Imagine a girl like you being offered two horses in one week. I never heard of such a thing."

Her father said, "You just took a load off our minds. I wasn't exactly looking forward to your riding that hot-rod Holiday all the time."

But somehow they weren't as enthusiastic as she had thought they would be.

"You're one lucky girl," said her mother in an

ordinary tone, "to have a horse like that just handed to you."

At the barn Middie went through the motions of grooming Holiday, but strangely there was no joy in it. She was excited about Jiffy, but she hadn't realized how hard it would be to say good-bye to Holiday.

Mrs. Bailey seemed resigned about the decision. "But that's entirely up to you, Middie. You're the only one who knows what you want most." But Middie couldn't tell her that what she wanted most was to have her family think as much of her as they did of Laurie.

Mrs. Bailey wouldn't phone Halsey — she said Middie would have to tell Halsey herself. Middie was going to phone him at noon. She was hoping Halsey could take Holiday away before the Mitchells brought Jiffy over on Sunday.

This was the last time Middie would ride Holiday. She wanted it to be a good ride, but Holiday knew something was wrong. She had to struggle with him at every step. He stiffened his jaw, tossed his head up, and bent his neck the wrong way. He even jumped up and down and threw a little temper tantrum.

Mrs. Bailey called out, "Why don't you put him away and not try to ride him one more time. You're upset, and it's catching."

Middie pretended not to have heard. She wasn't going to let her decision about Jiffy keep her from riding Holiday one last time. She asked him to canter.

Holiday picked up speed and shook his head, trying to jerk free. Middie swung him hard toward one of the jumps. I'll work him out of it, she thought. Too late she saw she had brought him in all wrong to the fence, and she braced herself for the refusal.

She was catapulted over the fence. Middie felt the horse tuck and twist under her in a supreme effort to clear the top bar. She flew off over his head as he landed. She heard Janet scream. She sensed rather than saw the horse leap clear over her as she hit the ground. Her face and stomach ploughed a long furrow in the dirt.

Silence. Middie rolled over on her back, struggled for breath, and looked up. All she could see was dust rising, billowing above her like a mushroom cloud. She blinked.

I wasn't listening to him, thought Middie. I didn't hear what he was trying to tell me. I wasn't thinking of him at all. He knew something was wrong, and I was so pigheaded . . . all I thought about was making him do what I said.

She started to run her tongue over her lips and discovered her mouth was full of dirt. She turned her head aside and spit, then looked back up at the dust cloud.

Whoever rides Holiday will always have to listen to him, she thought. Feel what he's feeling, and try to tell him what to do. She swallowed. I

mean, figure out how to make him *want* to do it.
He'll be like this the rest of his life. He'll never
jump that gully. Or a ditch jump. There're a lot
of things he'll never do, no matter how much time
I spend riding him.

The sky began to reappear in patches through
the settling dust.

But Jiffy . . . thank heavens Jiffy is different.
All I have to do is point him at the fence and he'll
take it. He'll do everything right. I'll be like Janet
on Minaret, winning championships. Laurie will
be proud that I'm her sister.

Her head was throbbing, and suddenly Laurie's
words were part of the throbbing. They went over
and over, like a needle stuck on a record. "You
never take the time to do anything right." She lay
there with the words pounding through her head.

As the air cleared, so did her mind. She knew
with certainty what she really wanted, even more
than admiration from her family. She had thought
that choosing the right horse was easy, but she
had almost made a terrible mistake.

First Janet and then Mrs. Bailey appeared beside her with worried faces. Slowly she got to her
feet and began brushing the dirt from her clothes.

"I'm okay, really," Middie said. "Just awfully
dirty." She went to Holiday and picked up his
reins. "I'll tie him up for a few minutes. I want
to phone Mrs. Mitchell about Jiffy."

"You mean phone Halsey about Holiday," said
Janet.

"No, I want to tell Mrs. Mitchell no thanks, she'll have to find someone else to give Jiffy to," said Middie. "I'm going to take Holiday."

They stared.

Janet exclaimed, "She's hit her head and she doesn't know what she's saying."

"Oh, yes, I do," said Middie. "Jiffy's awfully well-trained. He's a wonderful push-button horse. When I ride him, I can be a passenger and I won't have to work hard. I can keep on riding the way I do now."

"My best friend's gone off her rocker," moaned Janet.

Middie began to smile. "But when I'm riding Holiday, I can't ever just sit there. I'll have to work hard and ride him every second. I want to be a really good rider someday. Holiday can teach me a lot of things I need to know."

"Well!" said Mrs. Bailey. "Well, now!" She tilted her head, and Middie thought her face had a kind of glow on it.

"Besides, Holiday needs me as much as I need him. He's awfully sensitive, and he needs a rider who loves him a lot. Like I love him."

"You're insane," sputtered Janet. "Your best chance to have a real jumper and you blow it! What will people think of you if you never win anything?" She looked hard at Middie. "What will Laurie think?"

Middie shook her head. "I just figured out that what *I* think is more important. I'd rather be a better rider than try to impress my family with horse show ribbons. I have to learn a lot to ride Holiday." She saw the anxious look on Janet's face. "Honest, Jan," she said gently, "I'll be happier with Holiday, even if I never ride him in another horse show."

Janet shook her head. "That's not what you used to say. You sure changed your mind." Her face slowly cleared. "But if that's what you really want . . ."

"That's what I really want." Middie felt the smile spread over her face. She felt good — really good. "Tell you what — why don't you send me a picture of you and Minaret winning at Westchester? Even if I never win anything, I can show people I'm best friends with a championship rider."

Janet smiled wistfully. "Okay." Her face brightened a little. "I'll send you an eight-by-ten color print. Autographed and framed!"

Middie grinned and ran up the steps of the house to telephone. She carefully dialed the number of Highgate Hills Farm.

Mrs. Mitchell was surprised at first, and then very understanding. "I should have known you'd want a challenge. Don't worry about a home for Jiffy. Mike said if you didn't take him, we could offer him to Susie."

"That's super!" Middie exclaimed. "He's just what she needs! She'll love him!"

Mrs. Mitchell laughed. "About the Happy Valley Hunt Club — we'll send you an invitation to Opening Day just the same. I'm sure you and Holiday will have a lovely time."

Middie hung up the phone. Janet and Mrs. Bailey had come into the room. "Listen to this!" shouted Middie. "I'm invited to go on the fox hunt anyway, with Holiday!"

"I hope they don't have any ditches," said Janet.

"Fox hunt! Fox hunt!" chanted Middie, dancing around the room.

Janet gave her a look of disgust and went to gaze out of the window. She shrieked. "Derry got out! He's attacking Holiday!"

"How did Derry get out?" asked Mrs. Bailey, hurrying to the window.

Middie felt numb. The chain. She had forgotten to check the chain on Derry's paddock.

Janet pointed, "They're fighting! Holiday just broke his tie rope. Oh! *Oh! OH!* Look at Derry kick!"

Middie didn't hear her. She was racing to the barn.

25.
Derry Gets Even

Middie shouted at the horses as she ran. "No! No! Stop it! Stop fighting!"

She climbed the fence and hesitated. A cloud of dust billowed around the two horses as they reared and bit and struck at each other with their forelegs. Holiday's teeth opened a gash on Derry's shoulder. Derry whirled and kicked with both hind legs. Holiday reared in time, and Derry's hooves flashed by harmlessly.

"Stop that! Derry, get out of there!"

Both horses whirled again, and Derry kicked hard. Middie heard a thunk of hooves connected with solid flesh. Derry spun and galloped away.

Middie leaped from the fence and grabbed Holiday's broken tie rope. "Come *on*, Holiday! Let's *go*!"

She jerked and pulled, but the big chestnut flared his nostrils and stood planted. He trumpeted a challenge.

Derry whirled and came charging back. Middie grabbed a small rock and threw it at him as hard as she could. He hesitated. "Stop that! Derry, get out of there!"

Middie yanked with all her strength and this time dragged the reluctant Holiday into his paddock and slammed the gate shut. Then she climbed the fence to catch Derry. The two horses trotted up and down, snorting and glaring at each other, their ears flattened and their necks arched.

Derry didn't want to be caught. At last Middie got a tie rope around his neck and pulled him into his own paddock. She chained the gate and went back to Holiday. He was snorting and rolling his eyes so the whites showed.

"Are they all right?" asked Janet from outside the fence.

"I don't know," said Middie. She snapped another tie rope on Holiday's halter and led him to the tie rail. "I'm afraid Holiday is limping. They're both cut up a lot." She looked carefully at Holiday as she took off the saddle. "He's favoring his right hind."

Mrs. Bailey had hurried down to the barn after the girls. She examined both Derry and Holiday. "That slash on Derry's shoulder looks worse than it probably is; it will heal all right. They've both been kicked, but Holiday's is worse. Let's have a closer look."

Above the hock, inside, was a large curved cut with blood pulsing down the leg. Janet shuddered and turned away. Middie ran for the gauze and pressed a large pad over the cut.

"It's a good thing Derry wasn't shod," said Mrs. Bailey. "Let's hope it isn't very deep."

"I'll wash it with Betadine and put that yellow salve on it when it stops bleeding. Do you think he'll be okay?"

"With a kick like that, he can't be ridden for quite a while. They'll both be stiff and sore tomorrow. I don't understand how Derry got out."

"It's my fault," said Middie, looking down at the ground. "When we went to Highgate Hills yesterday, I was in a hurry and I didn't double-check the gate. If only I'd come back."

"If only. If only." Mrs. Bailey's voice was hard. "Unfortunately, it's the horses who have to pay for your carelessness."

"Oh, Mrs. Bailey, this is awful."

"Yes, it is. You can be thankful they're not hurt worse." Mrs. Bailey turned sharply and headed back to the house.

Words won't do. Middie began to treat the horses, washing their wounds with disinfectant and dressing them with ointment. Tears ran unchecked down her face as she worked. Holiday had many kicks and bites and skinned places as well as the large cut above the hock. Derry's injuries were fewer, but deep. Holiday's iron shoes had left their mark.

"I don't blame you, Derry," she said, dressing a raw place on his haunch. "No wonder you're jealous. I haven't given you nearly as much attention as I did before I got Holiday. But I'll be

177

better. I'll take the time. I'll brush you every day like I used to, and maybe Mrs. Bailey will let me lead you up the canyon when you're well."

Derry nickered softly and rubbed his head against her shoulder. She kissed his velvety gray nose and whispered, "I'm sorry. I'll show you I'm truly sorry."

She finished her work, put the jar back in the medicine chest, and sat down on a bale of hay. The barn was so peaceful, even though she knew the horses were hurt. She didn't want to leave them; she wanted to stay and comfort them. Comfort herself, really. The horses would forgive her for what happened if they knew she had caused it; horses were like that. But what would her mother say? Her mother didn't even know she had chosen Holiday.

She had said she would learn a lot from Holiday; the lesson today was a bitter one. She went up to the house.

"Are the horses okay?" asked Janet in a worried voice. "I can't stand seeing so much blood."

"I think they'll be okay," Middie said. "Let's go home. I have to tell Mom what happened."

"Uh-oh," said Janet. "She's not gonna like that."

"I can't help it. Let's go."

Janet gave a big sigh. "I wanted so bad for you to have a good horse, and you could have had Jiffy, but you chose Holiday. And now he's hurt, and you can't even ride him. Nothing's turned out the way I wanted it to."

Middie put her arms around Janet and hugged her. "That's okay. It's not your fault; it's mine. Things will work out, anyway, you'll see."

Middie had planned to straighten her room to make a place for Jiffy's ribbons. Why not clean it just for the sake of Holiday? It was something to do before her mother got home.

Her mother was late from work. Not a good sign, thought Middie. She watched her mother collapse into her favorite chair by the front window.

"Can I get you something to drink?" asked Middie. "Lemonade or iced tea?"

"Iced tea would be nice, dear." Her mother paused, looked at Middie carefully, and sat up straight. "What's happened this time?"

Middie said, "I hate to tell you. I forgot to check the chain on Derry's paddock, and he got out and got into a fight with Holiday."

"Oh, Middie! Are they hurt badly?"

"They're both kicked and cut up. But not too bad."

Her mother shook her head. "You certainly seem to cause more grief for everyone but yourself, sometimes." She sighed. "I really hope you'll be more careful when Jiffy is in the barn."

"Oh. I'm not going to take Jiffy after all. I'm going to take Holiday."

"You *what*?" Her mother looked shocked.

"I'm taking Holiday."

"You are *not* taking the Mitchells' horse?"

"That's right, Mom."

"But, why, Middie?" Her face showed pure astonishment.

Middie shrugged. "Jiffy's already trained, a push-button horse. Holiday will be better for me than Jiffy. It's going to take me a long time to learn how to ride him, but I want to learn. I want to be a really good rider someday." She went into the kitchen, dropped some ice cubes into a tall glass, and filled it from the big jug of sun tea in the refrigerator.

Her mother hadn't moved. She took the glass and said, "Mrs. Bailey told us you could learn a lot from Holiday, so we let you keep on riding him. But you're extremely competitive. You've always wanted to enter horse shows so you could win. Janet tells me you'll never win the kind of classes you like with Holiday, and Mrs. Bailey says she's probably right."

"I know, but I guess I realize that there are different ways of winning," said Middie. "Laurie can bring home all the trophies you want."

"Oh," said her mother. She sipped the iced tea, and a thoughtful look crossed her face. "Maybe you don't realize that Laurie hasn't much talent in tennis. She has to work awfully hard at it. That's why we're especially proud of her when she does win something. But, you, you're a natural in riding, and you never have to work hard. It's always come so easy for you."

Middie blinked. "Oh." She reached in her jeans for a tissue. "Well, I guess I just found out something about myself," she said. She blew her nose. "I have an awful lot to learn if I want to ride Holiday. And I guess that's more important to me than winning in horse shows." A grin wavered across her face. "I'll really have to work."

"I never would have thought . . ." Her mother sighed. Then she smiled. "Well, if you're going to be that serious, and take the time to do it, I suppose you'd better have new riding boots, leather ones. What do you think?"

"Mom! What do I *think! Leather boots!* Oh, MOM!" Middie leaned over her mother and hugged her.

"Watch out for my iced tea!" Her mother laughed and hugged her back.

"How can you be so nice to me when I've been so awful?"

"I don't know. Maybe I should see a psychiatrist."

"Maybe I should, too. I started cleaning my room."

Her mother looked stunned and then laughed. "I'll drink to that!" She lifted her glass high. "Cheers!"

Saturday morning Halsey stopped at Mrs. Bailey's house and gave Middie the ownership papers for Holiday. He inspected the horses. Derry showed no ill effects, aside from being quite stiff, but Holiday still favored his right hind leg.

"Don't you worry about him, girl," said Halsey. "He's a tough one."

Late Sunday afternoon, while Middie was sorting out the books on the shelves in her room, Mrs. Bailey phoned. She sounded very worried.

"Holiday isn't well, Middie. His leg looks infected. I think we'd better call the vet."

Middie swallowed hard. "Go ahead and call him. I'll be over as soon as I can."

26.
The Long Night

Middie and Janet hurried to Holiday's stall and stared. His right hind leg had swollen to twice its normal size. He stood listlessly with the hurt leg cocked, his head and tail drooping, and his eyes half closed.

Middie put her arms around his neck. "You're going to be all right, you hear? I'm going to stay with you until you get well."

Mrs. Bailey had phoned the vet. Middie began to think he would never get there, but at last his truck pulled up the driveway.

The vet examined the horse and shook his head. "Blood poisoning," he announced. "I'm certainly sorry. It's pretty serious. I'll give him a massive dose of antibiotics, but that's all I can do. We'll just have to wait and see. He's in bad shape."

"But he was all right last night," said Middie. "I thought he was all right this morning, though he didn't seem very eager."

Janet looked in his manger. "Why, he hasn't eaten any of his breakfast!"

The vet shook his head again. "Blood poisoning usually comes on pretty fast. Nothing to do now but wait. I'll stop by and give him another shot tonight." He turned to Mrs. Bailey. "Don't put him back in his stall."

"But it gets cold at night, and he's sick," protested Middie.

"Well, blanket him, but don't put him in his stall," repeated the vet, closing up the back of his truck.

"Why not?" asked Middie, desperate.

The vet looked at her kindly. "I'm sorry, young lady. If he goes down in his stall, we won't be able to get a winch around him."

Middie stared. The meaning of his words made her dizzy. She whispered, "You don't think he will get well?"

The vet shook his head. "I didn't say that. I just said . . ." He paused. "That's a mighty sick horse."

His truck disappeared down the drive. Middie watched him go with bleak eyes. She went to the tack room and brought out a heavy horse blanket. She buckled it on Holiday and turned to Mrs. Bailey.

"I don't want to go home, and I don't want any supper. Please, may I stay here? I can't leave him."

"Me, too," said Janet. "I don't want to leave Middie."

Mrs. Bailey said in a matter-of-fact voice, "Both

of you girls can have supper with me and spend the night. I'll phone your parents and ask. The guest room is always ready, and you're certainly welcome."

Their families said yes to the girls staying at Mrs. Bailey's.

After dinner, the girls fixed a bed of shavings for Holiday in the shelter of the barn and put the water bucket close by. Holiday looked at it, but didn't drink. Stars winked into the sky. Mrs. Bailey turned on the floodlight beside the barn. It made a small half-circle of comfort in the dark. A gust of wind blew down the canyon, and the girls shivered in their jackets.

"I'm going up to the house to bed," announced Janet. "You'd better come, too. I don't want you to catch cold."

Middie shook her head. "I can't leave him when he's so sick. He needs me."

Janet said in a low voice, "If only you had chosen Jiffy. Don't you wish you had?"

"Never!" blurted Middie. "I'm going to stay here and *make* Holiday get well."

She settled herself in the shavings beside him. Each time he lay down, she hovered anxiously over him, and each time he struggled to his feet, she sighed with relief. Finally he lay down and would not get up. Middie could not get him to move.

"I won't leave you, fella," she whispered. She sat down cross-legged and squirmed and struggled until she got his head onto her lap.

Middie had never held a horse's head before, and she was surprised at how big it was. It rested heavily on her knees, extending over both sides of her lap. She crooned to the horse, even though he couldn't hear her voice, and stroked him while she studied his closed eyes, his limp and motionless ears, and his delicate nostrils moving with irregular breaths. Middie stroked his forehead, ran her fingers up and down his jawline, and scratched his chin. Once he blinked and nickered softly down deep in his throat.

The vet returned and gave Holiday his second shot of antibiotics, but left without any encouraging word.

Shortly afterward, Middie heard another car zoom up the driveway and footsteps approach. She shivered and peered into the darkness beyond the floodlight. It was Laurie. Middie braced herself.

"I thought so," said Laurie. "You're not sleeping in the guest room — you're spending the night out here with that horse."

"I have to, he's so sick."

There was a silence. Laurie said, "You sure do love him, don't you?"

Middie nodded. She was too miserable to speak.

Laurie had a bundle in her arms. "I brought you your sleeping bag and pillow. I figured you'd need them." She laid them down beside Middie. "There's an extra blanket, too. You'd better keep warm so you can take care of that horse, hear?"

Middie wanted to say thanks, but she was too close to tears.

Laurie studied her a minute and then sat down beside her on the shavings. "You know, I had you figured all wrong. You've always been so hot for horse showing, as if winning was the only important thing in your life. And then when you have a chance to own a horse that will clean up at shows, you go and choose a horse that practically needs rehabilitation. Mom told me it's because you're serious about wanting to be a better rider."

Middie nodded again.

"Well," said Laurie, "you sure have a lot of guts, choosing Holiday. That's the kind of choice that leads to the Olympics."

Middie found her voice. "Come off it, Laurie."

"I'm serious. I bet you'll be a famous rider someday, and I'll say, 'Yeah, but I knew her when she got so excited taking a really tricky jump that she went off course.' "

Middie looked at Laurie, and they laughed together.

"You always used to take the easy way out, but you've sure changed since you met Holiday. Here you are, sitting all night on the cold ground taking care of a horse you won't be able to show very much, when he's so sick even the vet said . . ." She cleared her throat. "Mom and Dad are really proud of you." She touched Middie's arm and stood up. "And so am I." She brushed shavings off her

187

jeans and started toward the car. "Take it easy, Caboose."

Middie couldn't help it. "Don't *call* me that!" she cried out. "I *hate* it. I hate being the tail end of our family, the one nobody wanted! I'm always a pain!"

Laurie stopped dead. "What do you mean 'nobody wanted'?" She walked back toward Middie. "You just weren't *expected*. I thought you knew!"

"Knew what?" Middie's voice was full of despair.

"When you were born, you made our family come out even. Keith and Karen. Me and you. That's why we call you Caboose. A freight train isn't complete without one. You made our family complete. Anyway, you're no more of a pain than anybody else's kid sister."

"Oh." Middie looked up at Laurie's smiling face. She tried the word out softly. "Caboose." A warm feeling started to spread inside her. "When you put it that way . . ." She paused. "But don't you hate me because you can't go to Cal Poly?"

Laurie sighed. "I don't *want* to go to Cal Poly; I want to stay at J. C. with David. We're going to transfer later." She put her hands in her pockets. In a hesitant voice, she asked, "Do you still have that oil painting you made me for my birthday?"

Middie cringed inside. "Yeah. It's in my room."

"Would you mind giving it to me? I'd really like to have it, for keeps."

"Oh," said Middie, looking up at Laurie. "You bet." She smiled at her sister. "Boy, you are something else."

Laurie smiled back. "Anyway, take care of that horse. And yourself, Caboose."

Middie watched Laurie retreat out of the circle of light. Middie heard the car door open, and Laurie's voice reached her through the darkness. "He'll get well, with you there." The door slammed, the motor started, and the car lights disappeared down the drive.

Middie put her head down and said to herself, I hope she's right. Oh, I hope she's right.

She laid out the sleeping bag beside the horse and wriggled into it. How comforting it was. Funny that Laurie would bring her the sleeping bag and blanket after what Middie had done to her at the birthday party. And Laurie wanted the painting, after all! How wrong she had been about her family. Thinking about them made her feel warm. The Caboose, she smiled to herself. It was nice being the Caboose.

A sharp wind rattled the leaves of the big oak, and the horse stirred. Middie sat up uneasily and crawled out of the warmth. She looked long at Holiday, and then unzipped the sleeping bag and draped it carefully over the horse. She wrapped herself in the remaining blanket, sat down on the ground, and put Holiday's head in her lap again.

Mrs. Bailey made her way to the paddock with another blanket and a thermos of cocoa. Middie saw her eyes flicker over the sleeping bag and the horse.

"I suppose you're telling him you're sorry he's sick," said Mrs. Bailey briskly.

"Yes," said Middie uncertainly.

"Well, don't," she advised. "Don't sound sorry for him. Animals always depend on your tone of voice and your actions to know how they are. Even if Holiday can't hear you, he can certainly tell if you're depressed. You'd better talk and act as cheerfully as you can."

Middie sipped the hot chocolate. It tasted good, but it didn't melt the ice at the bottom of her stomach. "You mean, I should tell him about the fun we'll have on the fox hunt when he's well?"

"Excellent!" said Mrs. Bailey. Her look warmed Middie where the hot chocolate couldn't. "You're helping him more than you know." Her voice was very firm. "Love has no limits to the wonders it performs." In the same tone, she added, "You'd better save at least one blanket for yourself."

"I will," said Middie, smiling faintly.

"Ha!" snorted Mrs. Bailey, and she went back to the house.

Middie's feet grew numb, but she didn't want to move. The horse seemed quieter now, and his breathing was more even. Middie stroked him gently and kept murmuring promises of galloping again in the country. "We'll have all kinds of adventures together," she told him. "There's a trail leading up into the mountains . . ."

She felt herself drift off to sleep in spite of her determination not to. Lower and lower her head drooped until it was resting on Holiday's. She slept.

She dreamed she was galloping Holiday over the hills with the night wind in her face. The path was steep, but the horse galloped up the hill with no effort at all. Billowing clouds and bright stars flowed past them.

Then suddenly she was back in the barn, pushing the wheelbarrow. The barn began to rock back and forth. "An earthquake!" someone shouted. The barn roof collapsed on top of her and pinned her down. Middie awoke, frightened, to find herself sprawled on the ground with everything black. She fought off the thing that was holding her prisoner.

It was the sleeping bag, and the earthquake was Holiday, getting up and shaking himself. His bulk loomed tall and dark above her against the pearl-gray dawn.

"Holiday!" shouted Middie, scrambling to her feet. "You got up! You're better!" She leaned against him, and tears of relief welled up in her eyes.

Mrs. Bailey and Janet came around the corner of the barn, Janet lugging a heavy bucket with a gunnysack over the top. Holiday swung his head toward them and nickered.

"Beautiful morning, isn't it?" said Mrs. Bailey.

Middie wiped her face on her sleeve and nodded.

Mrs. Bailey pulled off the gunnysack covering the bucket, and the aroma of hot bran mash floated into the clear air. Holiday nickered again. "I thought if his fever broke, he'd be awfully hungry."

Middie held the bucket in front of the horse, and he plunged his head eagerly into the mash.

"He really *is* going to get well, isn't he?" asked Middie.

"Without a doubt," said Mrs. Bailey. "Any horse who eats like that has a real interest in life."

Middie steadied the bucket for Holiday and looked at Mrs. Bailey with a kind of wonder. "I promised him that when he was well, we'd go galloping again in the mountains. And now we really will!" She straightened up. "You said it would be a real challenge to bring out the best in this horse. Well, now I have the chance. I don't care how long it takes, but I will."

"Hallelujah!" said Mrs. Bailey.

Holiday suddenly lifted his head from the bucket and nudged Middie, leaving a big smear of bran mash on her jacket. She grinned and put her head against his shoulder. She said softly, "And you'll bring out the best in me, too."

27.
The Fox Hunt

Through the shafts of sunlight among oak trees and sycamores rode the group of horsemen, their scarlet hunt coats flickering alternately with coins of sunlight and pools of shadow. A number of spotted hounds scrambled ahead of them, noses to the ground and sterns moving above the brush like short, white antennas.

Lined up behind the first horsemen were the rest of the hunters, resplendent in formal riding attire and mounted on braided and burnished horses. An ecstatic Middie, so happy she felt she could hardly breathe, trotted along in the last group on Holiday. Mrs. Mitchell had been true to her promise of an invitation to the hunt.

Middie had never known such a splendid day. Above them arched a sky of deepest blue. All around them the gold leaves of aspens and sycamores swam translucent in the sunlight, or fluttered down to add to the carpet of gold beneath their horses' hooves.

Holiday danced happily, bobbing his head and snorting.

"You're new to the hunt, aren't you?" asked a girl in a black hunt coat and velvet hunt cap, mounted on a small but sturdy bright bay horse. She looked younger than Middie.

Middie laughed. "How did you know?" She was too happy to be abashed.

"Because your horse is so excited. He's supposed to go quietly, like my horse. See what good manners she has? Her name is Lady Patrician. I call her Lady Pat."

"She sure is nice," said Middie, "but Holiday won't ever settle down like that. He used to be an Event horse or maybe even a steeplechaser, and he's always excited when he's out in the country."

The girl looked surprised and impressed. "A steeplechaser? Oh, boy! I'd like to see him go. Let's get away from the hunt long enough to do a little racing and jumping!"

Middie was shocked. "We're supposed to stay with the hunt and do just what the huntsmen tell us, or they won't invite us back. They're responsible for the guests and the juniors. This isn't a point-to-point; it's a fox hunt."

"I've gone off before to do some jumping, and they've never said anything." She giggled. "Maybe they didn't see me."

"Well, I'm only here for hill-topping. My horse

194

was awfully sick a short while ago, and I want him to take it easy."

"I suppose that's a good reason." She shrugged. "I wish they'd let me hunt instead of hill-top. This is my second year. I know all about hunting, and this isn't even a real hunt. They don't care how well I ride; it's because I'm eleven they won't let me go. They make me sick."

"They have a lot of people to look after."

"I can jump all the fences the huntsmen jump, and I can go as fast as they can, too. You wait and see. I'll get a chance to show them."

"Well, be careful," said Middie, making up her mind to keep away from the girl on the little bay. She joined a group escorted by two riders in pink coats, one leading the group and the other looking after stragglers and closing any gates left open.

Middie soon felt that hill-topping was in many ways more rewarding than being part of the hunt. They rode leisurely from crest to crest, watching the distant hunt in progress. Their escorts would point out where they thought the trail was laid and the hounds might next appear. Middie delighted in the panorama as they rounded each hill in turn and cantered across to meet the wildly galloping hunt. They would rein in their horses and watch the hunt go streaming by.

As her group picked their way down a rocky hill, a brown hunter with a blaze pulled up lame. "Probably a stone bruise," said one of the huntsmen. He offered to accompany the worried-looking woman rider as she led her limping horse back to the trailers.

The rest of them rode to the top of another hill, and Middie caught her breath at the countryside laid out at her feet. The farthest hill was alive with color and movement as the hounds and hunters raced across the slopes and in and out among the trees.

In the valley below, a few stragglers were crossing a shallow ravine to catch up, and on the hill to their right was the caravan of cars with the officials of the hunt and some spectators. Their escort began to lead the group carefully down and around the steep hill. Middie hung back to be the last in line — she wanted to be alone for a minute to imprint the picture forever in her mind. Faintly she could hear the bugle of the hounds across the valley.

Then there was another sound, like a strangled cry, far below her to the left. She turned and saw the bay horse with the young girl scramble out of the ravine at the foot of the hill and gallop madly off to the left, away from the hunt. The girl was still with the horse, but she was way out of the saddle and hanging on to one side. She ought to let go and drop off, Middie thought. The ground is so soft from the rain, she probably wouldn't be hurt at all.

As the bay horse galloped from shadow into sunlight, Middie caught the glint of something metal-bright near the top of the saddle. It looked like — it was! — the stirrup from the other side, with the girl's boot caught in it. She didn't dare let go of the saddle or she would be dragged.

Middie gasped, horrified. She looked around to see if anyone else had noticed, but the escort and the hill-toppers were out of sight. She alone had seen the accident. She cupped her hands and yelled frantically for help. There was no answering *halloo*.

Middie couldn't wait. She started Holiday plunging down the hill toward the runaway while her mind was spinning. She knew it was a wild idea, but if she could catch up to the girl while she was still holding on, Middie might be able to grab the reins of the bay and stop her.

Holiday leaped and bounded down the hill, snorting joyfully in his newfound freedom. Middie looked at the valley below as they galloped. If they went straight down and crossed the ravine where the bay had crossed, she would never catch up to them in time. She would have to cut across the hill at an angle to the left. The ravine was between them, but it was quite shallow, and there were lots of places where she could easily ride down in and back up on the other side.

Now she was down at the bottom of the hill and galloping along in the valley, angling in toward the ravine and the runaway horse on the other side. The girl had slipped farther down, but she was still hanging on with both hands. Middie could clearly see the boot caught in the stirrup. The saddle had slid to one side because of her weight, but it was now held in place by the breastplate. The girl still had a chance.

Middie urged Holiday on. She felt him flatten out and lengthen his stride. His hindquarters were like powerful pistons, driving them forward while the scenery raced past. She tried to study the ravine as they came closer. It hadn't looked very big from up above, but now that she was near, it seemed to grow bigger with every stride. They would have to keep going and look for a place to ride down in and across.

Now they were very close, and Middie could see the cut of the banks. Her heart began to sink.

How deep it was, and the banks were so steep! They might be able to slide down in, but how would they ever get back out? As they galloped, she began to pray, "Please let there be a place."

Just then, looking far ahead, Middie saw that the ravine turned sharply to the left across their path and went up into the mountainside. It cut them off completely from the runaway horse.

"Oh, no!" she gasped aloud. "Oh, no, not that!"

Holiday could never make that jump. When they reached the ravine, she would have to pull him up and watch the girl slowly lose her strength, let go, and be dragged. The bay was now so frightened by the burden hanging on her side that she wouldn't stop until she was exhausted.

Middie was crying now, the tears running partway down her face before being blown away in the wind. She was weeping for the young girl, weeping for Holiday and the fear that haunted him, weeping for her own helplessness.

The ravine was black with shadow. Middie kept her blurred vision on it and prepared to check Holiday. She couldn't wait much longer, or they would both plunge in.

Far away the girl uttered one long, despairing wail. The sound caught at Middie's throat. She knew now what people meant by a breaking heart, because she could feel hers breaking.

She knew Holiday couldn't help, but she loved him. She would love him forever. What was it Mrs. Bailey had said about love the night that Holiday had almost died? Into Middie's mind flashed the warm look on the old lady's face. She heard Mrs. Bailey say, "Love has no limits to the wonders it performs."

In rhythm with the galloping hoofbeats, the words rang through Middie's head. *Love has no limits*.

If love had no limits, she would not give up.

She reached forward and put one hand on the lathered neck. "Oh, Holiday, I love you," she said out loud. "Please trust me this once. You can do it if you'll try!" and in the same clear voice, "Dear God, please help my horse."

She shortened her reins and steadied the horse for greater impulsion. Holiday was alert; he had seen the ravine to their right as they galloped, but he showed no apprehension. He was watching the ground in front of him when Middie felt his muscles suddenly tense. At last he had seen where the ravine turned, and he could tell that Middie was going to ask him to jump it.

All the old fears flooded his mind. He remembered again the hot summer wind in his face and the smell of sage in his nostrils as his hooves thundered over the hard-packed ground. The boy on his back was so light, he hardly felt him at all. Ahead of them yawned the huge ravine, and he remembered launching himself into space.

Again he remembered the scream of terror in midair from the boy, and he felt the frightful jerk of the reins that twisted his head around and pulled him down. Instead of the prairie on the far side, the clay banks and dry rocks of the riverbed came rushing up to meet him. He remembered the crash and the pain and then nothing.

But the wind was not hot and burning; it was cool, and the hands were not the boy's hands. They were the hands of the girl who loved him, who had stayed beside him when he felt so hot and tired he didn't want to stand up, when he found he couldn't stand up. He remembered her hands moving over his aching body, reassuring him. The huge ravine gaped open before him, and the girl was driving him toward it, asking him, trusting him, loving him. He took a firmer hold of the bit and did not hesitate.

At the very edge he gathered his hind legs under him for the leap. The chasm yawned wide — wider than Middie had thought. Too late she believed she had asked the impossible. But they were already committed, and she looked up at the distant mountain, her hands light and yielding.

She felt the enormous thrust of the thoroughbred's full strength, and the chasm fell away beneath them. They seemed to hang in midair, and then the ground rose up on the other side, and Holiday landed squarely in the thick grass and raced on toward the runaway.

Middie, prepared for certain and painful death, took the shock of the landing in a daze. Then she saw the bay horse quite close in front of her, to her right and less than twenty yards away.

Holiday was laboring now, gasping and straining with every stride, but slowly he closed the gap. Middie steadied him when they were even with the bay and moved as close as she dared. She gathered the reins into her left hand, dug her fingers into the braided mane, and leaned out to the right. Holiday swung up against the bay, pushing her into an arc, and Middie grabbed the girl around the waist with her right arm as the two horses finished the circle and came to a jerky and shuddering halt.

The two mounts stood, heaving, white with lather, while Middie dragged the girl half up onto Holiday and reached over to release the boot from the stirrup.

The girl clung to Middie, sobbing, and Middie put both arms around her and held her tight. After a few minutes, she let the girl slide down on to the grass. Middie mopped her face on her sleeve and swung off her horse.

"You're going to be okay," Middie told the girl. "I don't know how you hung on for so long."

"I don't, either," said the girl between sobs. "I thought you would never catch up."

"That's what I was afraid of, too." Middie looked at their horses, gasping and shaking. "You stay here while I walk our horses. They're too hot to stand. You're okay. Look, here come some people."

Sure enough, the caravan of cars had driven back up the road and were parked above them. A jeep bumped down the hillside toward them, and people were running down from the cars. A group of huntsmen were galloping up from the valley behind them.

Middie slipped the reins over the horses' heads and began walking. Her legs shook, and she wanted desperately to sit down, but she couldn't until she knew Holiday was going to be all right. He plodded along behind her, sweat running from his belly and his legs, but his eyes were glowing. From time to time he reached forward and nuzzled Middie at the back of her neck.

A crowd of people surrounded the young girl, and another group hurried forward to catch up to Middie. And there was Mike Mitchell on his big liver-chestnut hunter, leaping off and taking the reins of the runaway horse from Middie's trembling hands. He fell into step beside her.

"I don't believe it!" he exclaimed. "I saw it with my own eyes, and I still don't believe it!"

Middie just grinned at him and kept walking.

Mike shook his head. "There wasn't anyone watching who thought he could do it. Or that any horse could do it. You were right. Holiday must have been a really great horse."

Middie stopped in her tracks and shook her head firmly. "No, I was wrong." She turned to Holiday and gently rubbed his forehead. "He never stopped being a great horse. Not ever. He just needed a better rider, one he could trust." She looked up at Mike. "I'm getting there. I've got a long way to go, but with Holiday as my teacher, who knows?" She flashed him a smile.

Mike grinned back at her, and they began walking their horses again through the sunlit grass.

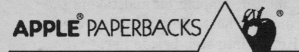